Red Clay Reader II

EDITOR

Charleen Whisnant

BOOK DESIGN

Maud F. Gatewood

PRODUCTION MANAGER

David Ramsey

**ASSISTANT TO
THE EDITOR**

Marge McDonald

RED CLAY READER *is published by Southern Review, a non-profit corporation
formed to support Southern writing.*

*Copies of the second collection available
at $3 each from the editorial offices lo-
cated at 2221 Westminster Place, Charlotte, N. C.*

RED CLAY READER *welcomes contributions
of money (patron, $10 or more—tax deduc-
tible) and manuscripts, but all unsolicited
material must be accompanied by return
postage.*

*Legal counsel: Haynes, Graham, and Bern-
stein, 1300 Wachovia Bldg., Charlotte,
N. C.*

EDITORIAL

Since the publication of RED CLAY READER in 1964, we've had some surprises. Who would have guessed that the first edition would sell out in three weeks, or that Harry Golden's affectionate description of southern liberals would have brought in responses of irrational anger?

We were not surprised by the deluge of manuscripts, for from the beginning RED CLAY READER has been motivated by a belief in the continuing action in the southern literary renaissance.

The experience of reading all these manuscripts has been a reassuring one; out of it has come most of the material for the second issue of RED CLAY READER. There are six writers here who have not been published previously and whose talent we wanted to encourage. There is also an indication in this issue of a trend we have observed in the fourteen months of reading. There have been various styles in evidence, many of them experimental, as if the writer has grown impatient with the limitations of single character, time, and mood that we have come to expect in short fiction. We have seen an extensive range in setting and symbol, but thematically the stories time and again are concerned with loss of illusion.

The evolution of this fact has led to speculations that literary markets are usually heavy with such exposures of loss while writers who attempt to construct tales of affirmation wind up in the widely circulated and more often compromised slick magazines.

The loss of indifference toward death, the realization that someone close to us and therefore we ourselves have got to die, is a trauma described by every new generation of writers. The southern writer seems especially taken with this topic, perhaps because he remains involved with older members of his family and is consequently exposed to the experience intensely and early. We have, however, had stories like this from all over the country. They are usually composed by writers in their twenties who because of their age have not had many emotional experiences except this one. More often than not, the description is poorly organized because telling the truth has dictated the inclusion of too much material. And yet it is possible to transcend the limitations of a stale subject as Charles East has done in the story, "Summer of the White Collie," published in this issue.

Aside from that typical and inevitable attempt to tell about facing death for the first time, we are also seeing writers wrestle to communicate the loss of other illusions. A bearded God who used to mete out justice from behind the clouds is gone. The image of ourselves as Americans, warm-hearted, clever, generous, noble savages loved by everyone, is gone. We sense, too, a depression over the population explosion. The homogenization of the world and the loss of individuality seem to be producing a nostalgia and a new emphasis on the regional aspects in fiction.

Perhaps the prevalence of this theme results from an acceptance of disillusionment as the most valid contemporary experience. Or perhaps it can be explained that most of us lose our sensitivity by the age of twenty-five; we become immersed in the everydayness of life and the satisfactions of materialism. Most of us outgrow the awareness that makes us vulnerable to the continuing loss of illusions. Those who do not, seem to be producing the fiction for RED CLAY READER.

CHARLEEN WHISNANT, *Editor*

Red Clay Reader

GATEWOOD

GEORGE GARRETT

When everything else is at best doubtful and always debatable I can't see any point whatsoever in ignoring the facts, such as they are. So here are the relevant facts. It is a fact:

(1) That the incidents herein recounted and speculated upon did take place in and about the small southern town of Paradise Springs. Population roughly ten thousand and declining. What once would have been called a "typical" town and is now a type only of the dead and wilting stalks left over from the vast Cornfield which was once America. Said Cornfield scheduled soon to vanish forever, to be covered with asphalt, painted arrows and parking slots, to become the biggest shopping center in the history of the world. Unless, of course, they succeed in blowing it up first. In which case it will be the biggest Desert we have ever seen, making the Sahara, the Gobi and so forth seem like piddling sandpiles.

(2) That there was, indeed, a double murder, the victims being one Alpha Burns, twenty-four years old, born and raised in Paradise Springs, and Daniel Lee Smithers, known as Little David, an itinerant revivalist preacher in his late thirties or early forties, but so small of bone and stature, so clear and unlined of skin and complexion, so pure and high of voice, that he might, with the aid of proper costume and a gold and curly wig, pass for a prodigy, a child chosen by the Lord and blessed with the gift of tongues and the healing touch.

(3) That two people were accused of, tried for, and convicted of the crime of first degree murder involving a conspiracy to commit a felony, to wit, to rob or steal or defraud from the aforesaid Alpha Burns $543.77, a sum which, for reasons which are not clear and not likely to be, she herself took from The Peoples Bank and Trust Company where she was employed as a teller.

(4) That these two people, now in custody and awaiting either eventual execution or the successful outcome of their separate appeals against the decision of the jury and the verdict of the lower court are (a) Billy Papp, alias "Goathead," born twenty-three years ago in Arab, Alabama, and in recent years successively employed as a short order cook, a used-car salesman, an undertaker's assistant, a carnival barker, and, of course, as general business and promotion manager of Little David Enterprises, Inc. And (b) Geneva Frond, aged 39; born in Yokum, Texas, raised and educated to maturity in a house of ill repute in Galveston; prospered briefly as a specialty dancer in such places as New Orleans, Newark, and Tijuana, Mexico, before some chemical change or glandular deficiency caused her to gain large amounts of weight which evidently, in spite of periodic weeping, praying, and fasting, could not be shed from her weary frame of bones; claimed to be the common law wife of the aforesaid Little David, which cannot be established as either true or false, but in any case taxes ordinary credulity due to her unusual size, Geneva standing well over six feet barefooted and weighing more than most professional football players during the banquet season.

(5) That no trace of the missing money has been found yet.

(6) That no one has been able to explain why the victim, aforesaid Alpha Burns, was both nude and bald as an apple at the moment of her unfortunate demise.

(7) That, in spite of a brief and prosperous invasion by reporters, cameramen, and curious tourists, life now goes on in Paradise Springs much as it did before these unhappy events took place, even gossip and speculation having faded now, the faint echo of human voices lost against the volume of noise and news of the moment; clamor is all and the rest is history.

2.
DARLENE BRUNK SPEAKS

I blame the whole thing from beginning to end on Penrose. I will blame him to my dying day. He knew we couldn't go without him and he took advantage. It was Penrose who started the whole thing. First of all he kept pestering us.

"Does he have snakes?"

We didn't know whether he had snakes or not and couldn't care less either.

"If he don't have snakes, I ain't going," he said.

I tell you I was getting sick and tired of that kid even if he was her brother. Him with his silly smirk and little peach fuzz of a chin beard. Skinny as a broomstick and all nervous with little jerks and twitches like a windup toy or a cockroach on its back trying to turn over.

I knocked him down and set on him and made him eat grass until he would promise to behave himself. But, being Penrose, as quick as he got up and out of reach, he took it all back. He ran off across the park, right across the public tennis court in the middle of a game, once around the bases of the softball diamond and then into the woods on the other side.

I wasn't about to give him the satisfaction of chasing after him. Alpha wasn't either. She sat down to rest in one of the children's swings. Alpha was tall, you know, but very delicate and lightboned. She could easily fit into one of those swings. She seemed kind of sad, so I gave her a few pushes and pretty soon she was smiling again. She got up and started pumping. She pumped so high I was afraid she was going to loop the loop and come down right on her head.

She checked the swing and when it slowed down she dropped off.

"I don't have on stitch one under this coat."

She smoothed the wrinkles out of the black raincoat she was wearing and pulled the belt tight around the middle.

"Sometimes I have trouble understanding you," I said.

"How could you?" she said. "I'm a virgin."

I call that a low blow, especially coming from your best friend in the world. But I wasn't about to let a cruel remark like that, probably just slipped off her tongue anyway, come between friendship or stand in the way of a good time. I wouldn't stoop to that.

"Well," I said, "I guess you'll be cool anyway."

And then we walked over to the woods and found Penrose in the tree.

3.
HOW PENROSE REMEMBERS IT

He is a way up there as high as he can climb, out on a limb looking down. They stand below looking up at him. He clears his throat to spit and they dance back out of range.

"I'm going to count up to ten," Darlene yells at him. "Then I'm coming after you."

"Start climbing."

She flutters her tongue at him, loud and rude. Then she slips off her high heel shoes and puts them down neat and side by side. She hangs her hat and gloves and pocketbook and stockings on a bush. She gets Alpha to unzip her and she wiggles out of that tight red dress. Then she spits on her hands and sizes up the tree. Amazing in bright red underwear.

Penrose thinks: *Here comes the Whore of Babylon if I ever saw one!*

In no time at all she is up there astraddle of the same high limb and facing him. He edges back out of reach, staring at the little silver cross she wears around her neck.

"What you looking at?"

"Guess."

"You ready to come on down and behave yourself?"

"What'll you give me?"

"I'll give you a quarter when we get down," she says.

"Sure, sure."

"Don't you trust me?"

"Not particularly," he says. "I gotta have security."

"People in hell want ice cream cones too."

She climbs down, very businesslike. Penrose smiles to himself and climbs down after her.

"I got a quarter coming."

Darlene opens her purse and hands him the quarter. Using the purse, she fetches him a head-ringing, sight-shattering, pin-wheeling pop that turns his knees to spaghetti and leaves him sitting on the ground.

He grins, shakes the cobwebs out of his head.

"It was worth it," he says.

4.
BILLY PAPP'S VERSION

Now that it has all come out I want to put down exactly what happened as far as I was concerned. I am going to tell the truth, the whole truth and nothing but the truth, so help me God.

If I told any little white lies in the court, it was only to protect others and because, being innocent, I did not realize the gravity of the situation. I did not have the slightest idea that I would end up waiting for the hot seat. I am a born optimist and always try to look at the bright side and that is probably how come I'm in the mess I'm in right now.

If I was as slick of an operator as they say, I wouldn't be here. If I was *that* slick, I never would have been working for Little David in the first place. There wasn't no money in it except what little I could pad onto my expenses. He may have been a spiritual man, I don't know. One thing for sure, though, he had a pretty fair idea of the value of a dollar and when he felt like it he could add and substract as fast as a machine.

I was a fool ever to fall in with him and the rest of his bunch. Don't that go a long way to prove I'm innocent?

I don't want to claim I'm an angel or something. And I'd like to take this opportunity right here and now to apologize sincerely for all those things I said to the reporters after the jury brought in the verdict. I was in a state of shock and not responsible. I know the trial was not a "joke" or a "frame up." No man in his right mind would ever call Judge Spence a "half wit" or "a dirty old man." I am especially ashamed of referring to my attorney, the Honorable John Rivers, Esq. as "a drunken bum who doesn't know how to try a law case." He done the best he could all things being considered. Every cloud has got a silver lining and now that I have come to my senses I can see that the trial was a very worthwhile and educational experience. I learned a lesson. And I'm going to prove it by sticking to the facts, telling exactly what I did and saw and heard. I'm not going to put down opinions and hearsay evidence.

Go back to the beginning. I left Little David and the rest of them working outside of Waycross, Georgia. Me and Geneva caught the bus and come on in to Paradise Springs a week ahead of time. Because it takes about a week of careful planning and arranging to build up interest in the show. It ain't like it used to be. Tent revival meetings has got all kinds of competition nowadays. Most people prefer to go to the drive-in theatre or watch the boob tube or maybe soak up a few beers somewhere. So what I usually do is hit a place early, slap up a whole lot of posters all over town, get in good with the law and the local merchants, meet folks, get around and present the right kind of an image. It's all part of my business. The reason I went most every night to The White Turkey is that it is reputed to be the most highclass honkytonk in Jefferson County and you got to go where the people go. And that's the same exact reason I would go down to shoot a few games at the Paradise Billiards Parlor. I wasn't doing it for the fun of it. Some got up and testified I was a hustler. That is not so. I admit I can sometimes shoot a pretty good game, but they were just sore losers. You know the kind I mean.

I usually work alone but this time Little David sent Geneva along with me, "to keep me honest," as he put it. He said he was worried about all my expenses. I told him he just didn't understand about inflation and the high cost of living. He said he would send Geneva along then to see about that. I replied that that was no way to cut down on expenses. He answered to me that two could live as cheaply as one.

The reason why me and Geneva registered at the motel as man and wife was so we could have one cabin and save money. There wasn't nothing between us. No kind of hanky panky. If I was fixing to shack up for real with somebody, Geneva would be the absolute last on my list. The reason why we registered under the name of Mr. and Mrs. Lincoln Vale of Everglades, Florida was not for the purpose of fooling anyone. We had had a few cans of beer at the last bus stop and we were feeling pretty good. And we had to put down *something* on the register or it wouldn't look respectable.

Okay. I was in Paradise Springs for one week. I put up the posters the first night. I spent the day time either doing business around town or shooting pool. And at night we would go out to The White Turkey and have a couple of beers and mingle around.

Now, this here Penrose Burns, the brother of the unfortunate deceased, he has testified that he knew me from the pool room. That may be so, but I did not know him from Adam. That is to say that he was just a pimply kid that was hanging around. The kind you would send out to get you a pack of cigarettes or a cup of coffee. I did not even know his name and didn't pay him no mind one way or the other. I was shocked and surprised when he showed up in court to testify.

And now, before going ahead with what happened on that fateful night, I would like once and for all to clear up any misunderstanding about my relations with Miss Darlene Brunk. I would never say anything to hurt a young lady's reputation and I would die with my lips sealed if I thought it would do any good. But so much has already come out during the trial that the only decent thing for all concerned is for me to tell the truth.

Yes, we did become acquainted at The White Turkey. As it happened she was without an escort, her date having passed out in the parking lot. She asked me to help her put him in the back seat so he could sleep it off and I did. She thanked me and offered to buy me a beer which is how we became acquainted.

When we sat down at the table Geneva started giving me a bad time and this was keeping me from getting decently acquainted with Miss Brunk. I did not know what Geneva might do or say. I was worried about the public image of Little David Enterprises and what might happen if there was a scene. And that is the only reason I put a few drops of medicine, what the Prosecutor kept on calling "a mickey," but which was actually a mild tranquilizer, into Geneva's beer while she was in the Ladies Room. Shortly thereafter, when she had come back to the table and killed the can of beer, she said she felt a little dizzy and wanted some fresh air. Which is the last we seen of her until later.

Miss Brunk seen me put the stuff in the beer can and she did not say or do nothing or register any known form of disapproval.

I was not lying when I told Miss Brunk that I was in the show business, I was, I admit, exaggerating a little when I implied to her that I was a talent scout. However, my experience in the carnival had taught me how to recognize a genuine talent.

I offered her an audition sincerely and I honestly thought she took my offer in the spirit in which it was intended. I was very surprised at what she said on the witness stand. I quote from the transcript:

Mr. Rivers

How long did you and Mr. Papp remain at The White Turkey?

Miss Brunk

Until they threw us out.

Mr. Rivers

Approximately what time was that?

Miss Brunk

Shortly after two o'clock in the morning. They stop serving at two.

Mr. Rivers

What did you do after, as you say, they threw you out?

Miss Brunk

I cannot recollect too clearly. I mean, there I was and I had been drinking beer pretty steady since around five o'clock. I guess I was a little high, as they say.

Mr. Rivers

Have you ever heard of The Hitching Post Motel?

Miss Brunk

Yes, sir.

Mr. Rivers

Isn't it a fact, Miss Brunk, that upon leaving The White Turkey you and Mr. Papp did go to the Hitching Post Motel and that you did spend the night with Mr. Papp in his motel room?

Miss Brunk

No, sir.

Mr. Rivers

Do you deny it?

Miss Brunk

Well, not all of it. Actually, see, we did not go to his motel room. He suggested that, but I refused.

Mr. Rivers

Miss Brunk, I caution you that you are under oath. . . .

Miss Brunk

Oh well, you probably know anyway or you wouldn't be asking. It's the truth, though. I would not enter his room that he had already paid for. I insisted that Mr. Papp rent another room for me and he did. He picked number 13 because I said it was my lucky number.

Mr. Rivers

Why did you go to the motel with Mr. Papp?

Miss Brunk

He wanted to give me an audition . . . .

Judge Spence

Order! Order in the court!

Miss Brunk

He stated to me that he could help me get ahead in the show business. I stated to him that I had already had a bellyful of that when I was a singer with the band at the Mickey Mouse Club, before they closed it down. And he stated to me he wasn't talking about anything small-time like that.

Mr. Rivers

Did you honestly believe that Mr. Papp intended to hold an audition in room number 13 of The Hitching Post Motel?

Miss Brunk

I had my doubts.

Mr. Rivers

But you went anyway.

Miss Brunk

I didn't have anything else to do at the time.

Mr. Rivers

And did Mr. Papp give you an audition?

Miss Brunk

Well, when we got inside, he stated to me that it was probably a little late for a singing audition and that it would be a shame for us to wake up the neighbors. So we discussed the situation awhile and then he suggested that I could do a hoochy-koochy dance.

Mr. Rivers

A hoochy-koochy dance?

Miss Brunk

You know. It's where you just kind of dance and shake around a little.

Mr. Rivers

Would you call that a legitimate test of talent?

Miss Brunk

Well, sir, some girls can do it and some can't.

Mr. Rivers

Did you perform this dance to music?

Miss Brunk

It was too late to turn on the radio. So he put some cellophane over his pocket comb and hummed through it.

Mr. Rivers

After this so-called audition why didn't you get dressed and go home?

Miss Brunk

I figured as long as I had gone that far I might as well spend the night.

Mr. Rivers

Did you sleep together?

Miss Brunk

There was only the one big double bed. I wasn't going to sleep on the floor for no man.

Etc. Etc. Etc. Miss Brunk made me look pretty bad in the court and everybody had a good laugh at my expense. Mr. Rivers cleverly got her to admit she accepted money from me the next morning, but she turned that around to prejudice my case too. First, he asked her if she knew that by accepting money she was behaving like a common prostitute.

"I am not a prostitute," she said, "and I have never done anything *common* in my whole life."

"Why did you ask for money, then?"

"I hardly knew Mr. Papp. He was a stranger in town and I wanted to impress on him that a stranger couldn't take liberties with a local girl just for the fun of it."

"You were thinking of his good and the good of the community."

"That is correct."

And that was the last time I seen Miss Darlene Brunk until she showed up knocking on the trailer door. It is true that I phoned her a couple of times, but only as a common courtesy.

Now then, we get to the night the murder took place. Here is exactly what happened as I witnessed it.

(1) I sold the tickets of admission and we had a very big crowd. I had hired three off-duty cops to handle the traffic and in case there was any rough stuff. And also because the Chief of Police suggested it would be the thing to do. Right after the service was over I paid them off in cash just in case they wanted to leave for some reason. I was feeling pretty good because I knew it would be a big collection. I don't mind losing a little sleep to count money.

I started for my trailer. I was going to settle down with a pint and wait until time to count up the collection.

Anyway, I get to the trailer and there is the kid, that Penrose, waiting for me. He said he wanted his money back because there weren't going to be any snakes like it said on the poster. I explained to him that it was against the law in this state to play with the snakes. He stated to me that if I didn't give him his money back, he would go tell a cop some cock and bull story about how I was trying to "molest" him.

"Aren't you a Christian, kid?"

"Don't give me that," he replied. "I walked all the way out here to see snakes and I want my money back."

I took a look around. It was dark and nobody was near. I thought I'd like to be fair to the kid, but at the same time he needed to learn a lesson before he got himself into real trouble.

"I guess you got a point," I said, fishing in my pocket.

And the greedy little runt came right up to me with his hand out and big grin on his face. All I did was wipe that grin off with the back of my free hand. But he fell down and commenced to holler and carry on. Naturally I wanted to quiet him down. If somebody came along there could easily be a misunderstanding.

I gave him a quarter to shut up.

"It was an accident," I said. "I didn't mean to hit you a lick like that."

"Don't flatter yourself," he said. "My sister can hit harder than you."

He took off before I had a chance to take the quarter back.

When the collection was all in I took the money to David's trailer and was going to count it and put it in the safe. Then it occurred to me that with such a big collection, the most in months, there might be a danger of robbery. You never can tell. That is the reason I took the safe over to my trailer. It would be safer there. And that is the only reason I had the gun.

About the nigger. Raphael Cone has been with us quite a while. When we work with a nigger audience or an integrated crowd we use Raphael as part of the program. He is educated and can preach. Other times, such as in Paradise Springs, he just helps with the equipment. As it happens he was also supposed to keep an eye on the crate containing the snakes.

I do not have any prejudice at all. One man is the same as another to me. But I'd be lying if I didn't admit to you that personally I did not get along with Raphael. He got more money than he deserved because he could preach. I may not have any education to speak of, but I could have preached too if they had ever given me a fair chance. The one time I did was on short notice and that was a bad unruly bunch of rednecks. They were looking for trouble and I don't think they would have listened to the Lord Himself. But Little David blamed me for the damage and took it out of my salary too. So naturally I was inclined to dislike Raphael. I'll admit it was silly to call him Rastus all the time. I called him Rastus Coon, trying to provoke him. But he was a slick operator. He would just smile and ignore me. He tried to get even in little ways. Like wearing those bermuda shorts and knee socks. The sight of him strutting around in bermuda shorts would outrage any man, even me. It was like he *wanted* to make me have a prejudice. Sometimes he even smoked a pipe.

Well, there I was in the trailer. I had the safe open and the gun in plain sight and I was transferring the money from the safe into my suitcase because I figured that if anybody tried to rob us they would never look there. And wham-bam, Rastus walks right in without knocking. He didn't give me a chance to explain anything.

"What's the big hurry?" he said.

It was my honest opinion that he thought I was trying to rob the money and that he wanted to be cut in for his share. Which is why I pointed the pistol at him and threatened to shoot him. Of course, I had no intention of shooting anyone, but knowing that they scare easy I thought it would save a whole lot of long-winded explanation. Which it did because he took off running.

I was just getting started again, transferring the money to my suitcase, when here came Miss Darlene Brunk, all upset about something. She said her best friend had flipped her wig and given away a lot of money she shouldn't have. She said she had to get it back. She would do anything to get it back.

"Anything?"

"Yes," she said. "You name it."

So I suggested that she meet me at The Hitching Post later and we could work out some kind of an arrangement.

She said that would be all right.

The service still had a while to go, so I gave her a drink out of my pint and we got to talking. I was only kidding, *testing* so to speak, when I suggested that she take the suitcase to The Hitching Post and wait for me. I wasn't serious but I wanted to see how serious she was. I did not think Miss Brunk would become involved in what looked like crime unless she and her friend were in real trouble. When she said she would go so far as to assist me in stealing the money—which, as I say, I had no intention whatsoever of doing—I knew that she must be serious enough.

I still had time to kill before the end of the service and was getting a little bored just waiting around, so I suggested to her that, as long as she didn't have anything else to do, she might do me a quick dance.

I turned on the transitor radio and she started in dancing. She was in a hurry to get back to the tent so she couldn't really concentrate on her performance. But even so it wasn't too bad.

Well, with the air-conditioner on and the transitor playing rock and roll and me concentrating on her performance, I wasn't paying much attention to anything outside. Next thing I know Geneva busts into the trailer. She takes one look at Miss Brunk and makes some kind of a sarcastic wisecrack. And I asked her what did she think my trailer was, The Grand Central Station?

"Gimme your gun, quick!" she says.

And, being so surprised, like a fool I give it to her. She took it and started to leave.

"Anything wrong?"

"Not much," she says. "The snakes are loose in the tent and the tent's on fire and David has gone crazy. That's all."

Miss Brunk grabbed her clothes and took off. I ran after Geneva, trying to do my duty during an emergency.

People was rushing hither and yon and I was delayed. Time I got to the trailer there was Geneva with my gun in her hands and the other two just a lying there deader than a couple of mackerals. Then the police come in and didn't give anybody a chance to explain anything.

Now, I realize that Miss Brunk sat up there on the witness stand and denied outright that she ever come to my trailer and done any dance. And I realize there is no proof she was there. Except my word of honor. I try to be a gentleman and I wouldn't even mention it now if my life didn't depend on it.

Now, about the money. All I know is it was still there when I left the trailer. So somebody had to take it. It couldn't have been Geneva. It *could have been* most anybody in all the confusion. But they was only two who *knew* about it. I do not believe Miss Brunk would have taken it. She was probably out there in the dark trying to get dressed. If she had been running around the trailer somebody probably would have noticed her.

That leaves only you-know-who, Mr. Rastus Coon. And I've got more than just suspicions. For one thing there is the dime. When they opened the suitcase all they found was one dime. A normal person would take it all or, if they was in a hurry, leave bills and change all scattered around. Rastus would leave me a dime just for a joke. Very mean that one, and smart too. Remember how he acted in the trial. Like an old-time "darkey." He showed up wearing overalls and he never wore a pair of overalls in his life. And all that "yassuh" and "no suh." Pully-wooly and "I rekcon this old shine just don't rightly recollect." The jury loved him. And they actually took *his* word against *mine*.

Whoever wants to find all that money will have to find Rastus first. Just go to some place like Paris, France, and look for a nigger in bermuda shorts smoking a pipe. He's probably there right this minute, drinking champagne and wine and laughing his head off.

He better laugh while he can. As soon as I get out of this situation, I'm coming after him. I just hope he hasn't spent it all already. But you know how they are about money—here today and gone tomorrow.

5.

BRIEF EXCERPT FROM SECRET DIARY
OF PENROSE BURNS

What happened after we got to Revival Meeting.

(1) Quick as we got inside I slipped out. Figured they'd never miss me anyway. Figured correct.

(2) Went to Papp to get money. Got quarter.

(3) Walked 1/4 mile to Texaco Station. Broke quarter. Drank kingsize Dr. Pepper and ate bag of peanuts for supper.

(4) While there sneaked under station wagon with yankee license plate. Loosened radiator drain cock where it would fall out a few miles up the road in middle of nowhere.

(5) Headed back up edge of highway toward tent. Dropped trousers and threw a moon at Greyhound bus going south.

(6) Took a look around, hunting for snakes. Saw Papp carrying safe to his trailer.

(7) Found nigger sitting on crate of snakes smoking pipe. Told him Papp said it was emergency, to come to his trailer as quick as he could.

(8) Removed crates of snakes nigger had been sitting on.

(9) Saw nigger take off across field. Laughed like hell at him. Nigger stopped long enough to hit me with rock the size of golf ball in pitch dark. Lesson— *keep moving when laughing in dark.*

(10) Saw Darlene go to Papp's trailer.

(11) Dragged crate over to trailer window to stand on.

(12) Watched Darlene do hoochy-koochy. Silly.

(13) Dragged crate to edge of tent. Opened it and dumped out snakes. Snakes groggy. Got some posters. Lit same and applied to snakes to make more lively. Snakes got going into tent. Tent caught fire.

(14) Moved back and hid in dark to observe commotion. Laughed fit to kill.

(15) Observed Little David go into trailer. Was going to take crate to stand on and spy on him. Then saw Alpha run in same trailer.

(16) Rolled in dirt and ripped my shirt. Started crying. Ran and found cop. Told him Little David

beat me up and him and Papp had my sister locked in a trailer. Cop run off toward trailer.

(17) Heard shots. Figured it was cop.

(18) Sneaked to Papp's trailer. Took off shirt to use to hold money from suitcase. Took all money. Left him dime. Change from quarter.

(19) Also found Darlene's silver cross on floor. Took it.

(20) Run home through woods. Hid money in secret place.

(21) Home just in time to hear sad news about Alpha. With cops stuck to story.

(22) Finally got to bed and slept good.

(23) Don't have slightest idea what Alpha was up to.

(24) Money safe and sound until needed.

(25) Silver cross is only proof Darlene was in Papp's trailer. After trial told her had seen her and had silver cross to prove it. Wear silver cross around own neck.

(26) That's about all I know and all I had to do with it.

6.

SIGNS OF GLORY FOR ALPHA BURNS

Scissors flash bright click click & hair falls snip-snip
Close eyes won't look
He will next shave my skull like his bald cool
smooth clean
Just like a nun
Just like women after war
Then
Then will act if ever

He cuts her hair as she asked him to and she closes her eyes knowing the time has come to act.

On the way to work, after a night of puzzling dreams, she saw the posters. Bright red they were with large black letters.

OLD TIME TENT REVIVAL

SINGING AND PRAYING

PREACHING AND HEALING

It went on to tell of the additional entertainment offered by the child revivalist, "Magic Tricks and Illusions/Secrets of the Ancient World/Bring the Whole Family." At the bottom of the poster was a photograph labelled THE FABULOUS LITTLE DAVID IN PERSON. A boy-like man in short pants with loose shirt and wide collar. He wore what could only be a wig, long, curly, and golden. Beautiful hair, like the princess' in a fairy tale. Bright and staring eyes.

He had great power, she could tell. She had power too, though, the power of her dreams which were sent to her by God. She knew at once, when she stared into the eyes of the photograph, that this was a test at last, that the posters were a sign. He with his tricks and illusions, his power of healing, he could change everything here into something new and strange. Briefly that would seem a blessing. Like a magician with his rabbits and doves, flashes and fires and puffs of smoke, he would dazzle his congregation right out of their cages of suffering skin and bones. They would be lightened, uplifted, empty and contented. Yet he would be gone. And they would be left, slowly to lose the vision of magic and slowly to rejoin their company of ghosts, sorrows, and secrets, only, don't you see?, poorer, the worse for wear now. For now they would have a need for visions. They would starve from a new hunger. And the whole of God's created world would blur and fade like an old photograph. And then having lost the beauty and solace of the real world that God had made, wouldn't their natural sufferings be compounded, always accompanied, like music in the movies, by the steady sound of lewd, demonic laughter?

She knew that the Creation was good and that this one great truth outweighed all arguments and all evidence. Not only suffering in all its rich and various forms but also all human action, good or evil, were weighed in the balance and, lighter than dust, weighed nothing. Nothing, therefore, was imperative, nothing was commanded of her except that, of course, she alone must cherish this truth. Having been so chosen, she must preserve herself for this cause.

And it would be within her power somehow to change everything too. Not by deception. Not by the dazzle of dissatisfaction. But by doing something so wonderful that the scales of their eyes would fall away and quite suddenly, old or young, rich or poor, lucky or losers, they would all see Paradise Springs as it really is—not commonplace or known at all, but marvelous, stranger than China or Persia in old books, and above all beautiful, world without end.

Even before she had finished staring at the poster a boy on his way to school paused briefly to draw a big mustache on the face of Little David. Only he was too late to spoil anything now, for, looking into his eyes, she had already been granted a vision, a bright glimpse of her own power and her duty.

Her friend, Darlene, who for all her wild behavior, served almost as a testament, a living sign of the Truth, who was rich in health and body as the earth itself and likewise always giving and giving without regret, Darlene would go with her.

"He's just a kind of an overgrown midget," Darlene said. "But you know me. I'm game for anything."

Alpha kept thinking about the face in the photograph, trying to know it so well that she could, anytime she wanted to, close her eyes and see it clearly. A face at once hurt and cruel, hard and fixed like the face of a ventriloquist's dummy. Yet somehow speaking. Without words, without expression, with no gesture still saying "I know. I have seen hell. I see it now and always. I carry hell with me. It is here and everywhere else." It was only the last part that was the Lie. She knew hell from her dreams.

So during the week she continued her usual life, going to work, wearing her own blank mask of a face, as always, mechanically and efficiently doing all the things she had to do. Not planning anything yet, just waiting patiently. With diplomacy and patience she was able to convince her parents to let her go to the revival.

Her father. He with his bum, gimpy leg left over from the War. With his big fist forever shaking at the stars and into the faces of the fools and knaves who populate the world. He ridiculed the God which the knaves had invented for the fools, had first invented and then killed, then dispossessed of what should have been His own by sending Him off to live in the blue sky somewhere, lonesome and far from His Creation. Her father limping to and from the post office to pick up his pension check, the rest of the time sitting grimly in his high-backed rocker on the front porch, just watching the fools and knaves hurrying to and from their separate, shabby little dooms; or else at the big kitchen table in another mood, cleaning and caring for his collection of rifles and pistols and shotguns,

preparing, not grim now but gaily, for the inevitable day of reckoning when at last the U.N. and the Supreme Court would dare openly to fly the hammer and sickle flag and the Combined Operations Forces of niggers, commies, jews, and catholics would take over the U.S.A. Which, he estimated, they would do easily enough and without any real resistance. Except for one small Surprise. Except for a small frame house in an obscure town, a house with a shady patch of unkempt yard, a house needing a new coat of paint, where one old soldier, bum leg and all, would be waiting heavily armed and able to make them at least earn his living space in blood.

Her mother. Who, maybe in spite of and maybe to spite, keeps her mouth shut, her lips zipped together like a thin, pale scar, saying nothing on these subjects. Goes regularly alone once a week to The Church of the Primitive Jesus beyond the edge of town, walks alone to and from that shabby building, keeping its secrets and solace to herself. Otherwise spends most of her waking hours hunched over her old-fashioned Singer sewing machine, bent and staring, squinting while the machine buzzes and the needle leaps up and down, making fine clothes with a good fit and at half the price of the stores. Bridal gowns and widows weeds. With the same skill and identical intensity making a dress for a first communion or clothes like Darlene's.

They agreed she could go provided that Penrose went along too, to look after them. Penrose with a choirboy face said he would be glad to go along and make sure the girls got there and back safe and sound.

By Friday all that was left was the sign. It came to her in the afternoon, praise the Lord. She was counting the money in her drawer at the bank when she heard a soft hissing noise. She looked and saw that all the bills had suddenly turned into little green snakes. They writhed and twisted in her hands. They were slimy to touch. She was going to drop them and run away, but then she realized it was a test and a sign and she gripped them so tight that her fingers were cold. When she had strangled the snakes, they turned back into dollars again.

Smiling and relieved, she counted the money and put it in her purse. In the locked bag which would be put in the vault she placed an I.O.U., listing the exact figure, promising to repay it as soon as possible at standard rates of interest, and adding, "I am borrowing this sum to offer it in sacrifice, to lay it upon the altar of Jesus for the purpose of doing His work in this wicked and unhappy world." She stuffed the bag with kleenex so it wouldn't look suspicious and then put it in the vault and went home. They wouldn't even find it until Monday morning and by that time she would have done her duty.

She wondered what she should wear, then realized that her uncertainty was a sign. She would slip her raincoat over nothing at all.

Which she did, stuffing the money in one pocket and her father's short barrelled .32 caliber revolver in the other.

7.
LETTER FROM GENEVA FROND TO THE GOVERNOR

I know you are a busy person with troubles of your own and so I will try and be brief.

But I don't hardly know where to begin or how.

One thing, I am sure I got a fair trial and the judge and jury done what they thought was right.

I know I have committed a crime and have to be punished for it. But still I swear before God and man I was not guilty of trying to rob that poor girl or of any conspiracy with Billy Papp.

A whole lot come out in the trial that I didn't know nothing about. A whole lot was news to me. And there was a plenty of things to laugh at too. I do not blame the people for laughing. I have been laughed at before and if I die in the electric chair somebody will be bound to laugh then. A big fat woman is truly a joke and it is already funny that they have to fix the chair all special for me and my size and weight. If they laugh I will not blame them because it is hard not to laugh sometimes even when you don't want to.

I am at peace with myself and my God and I do not mind their laughing any more. Laughter is God's gift. If it wasn't for that gift we would all be crying all the time.

That's what Little David taught me and it changed my life. One time I had been healthy and goodlooking. Some people thought I was even beautiful. At least they said so. And then I got this thing. The doctors couldn't figure out a name for it but I had it whatever it was and I just blew up like a balloon. And being a woman and all I was very hurt. I cussed everybody and everything and I hated myself. More than one time I tried to kill myself and disfigure myself. But I was even scared of the pain.

I was a lost soul.

Then I went to a revival healing because I would try anything. When I kneeled down, Little David put his hands on my head and he whispered to me that he couldn't make me thin and beautiful again but he could heal me.

I was mistrustful and suspicious but I went to him privately anyhow and he talked me into joining up with his group. And the way it worked was gradual but it worked. I would see all kinds of suffering and tribulation. And I seen how he suffered too, being so small and sickly and all. And after a while I come to realize that I didn't care that much about myself any more. I mean, little by little I stopped worrying about me, myself, and I.

And that's how I come to love him. I stopped hating me and started loving him and then he started loving me too and then it was a true glory for I was healed.

We was common law man and wife together and shared one roof. I know that people wouldn't believe that and even if they did it made them laugh to think of the two of us together. They just did not understand. I had been as my record proves a prostitute and a hard-living woman long before. And one thing I learned is that love and sex is not the same thing at all more often than not. What I mean is I wasn't no girl without no experience. I had a plenty of experience both good and bad.

I knew what I was getting into and I didn't care.

Nobody has a right to ask what went on between us. That is private. But I can say without being ashamed that I loved him and he loved me and that it was a real glory. There was times when I felt as light and frail as a girl again and he was a giant as big as a mountain. Nobody can take that from us alive or dead.

Now I want to tell how it happened that night. I have seen many a crazy thing in my lifetime and sometimes have wondered if I wasn't crazy myself but I have never seen anything like that night.

It is true I did notice that woman, the late Alpha Burns, because when I first passed the collection plate during the offering she reached right into her pocket and come up with more than fifty dollars in assorted bills and just plunked it in the plate, *deposited* it so to speak like it was trash, maybe a old candy bar wrapper or something. That is enough to make anybody take notice. She and her friend who was with her had an argument about giving all that money and her friend tried to snatch it back but Miss Alpha Burns wouldn't let her.

And naturally I did point her out to David.

Later on she come up front to witness and be saved and her friend wasn't with her. She put another wad of cash in the plate up there and then she spoke to me where I was just standing there holding the plate. She said she wanted to see David personal and private.

She did not act crazy. She was soft-spoken and looked sincere to me at the moment. And anyway she had just put so much money in the plate I couldn't refuse her. So I told her that since the service would be over soon anyway why didn't she come with me and I would show her the trailer where she could wait and see him.

That seemed to suit her fine and I took her to the trailer.

I better admit something since it can't do any harm anyway now. It wasn't the first time I took a girl to the trailer like that. In our line of work we depend a good

deal on kooks who will get moved by the spirit and give away some goodsize offerings. We never did actually discourage them. That may be wrong in a way but we had to keep alive. And naturally in the case of Little David, he had a way of getting kooky girls and women interested in him and his cause. Some of it was motherly and some of it was sick. But I would keep my eye open and be on hand in case anything went wrong. If I had suspected the girl was a *real* kook I would never have led her to the trailer in a million years. She appeared to be a sincerely religious person and that I guess is what fooled me.

We went inside the trailer and I turned on the lights and the air-conditioning to make it comfortable. While I was doing that she empties out her pockets on the bunk. I looked around and I seen a big pile of money and I also seen this pistol. I knew right then it was going to be trouble of some kind. But I didn't want to let on that I noticed until the right time.

"Are you comfortable?" I said to her. "The air-conditioning will cool it off in a minute or two."

"I'm fine," she said, "but I think I'll slip out of this old raincoat if you don't mind."

I said to myself Geneva, it's a crazy world and maybe you are crazy too but this one takes the prize and maybe you better get in high gear and warn David what's waiting for him.

I excused myself politely and started back. Only by that time the snakes had got loose and the tent was burning. Here came David running. He was all upset and crying and cussing and he wouldn't pay me no mind. He just shoved me out of the way and ran on towards the trailer.

Everything was going on at one time, and it is a wonder that I didn't just keel over with a stroke or a heart attack. I tried to catch my breath and think. I remembered that Billy Papp, he owned a pistol. I seen it in his suitcase at the motel. I figured I had better get it quick in case that girl was fixing to use her pistol for some mischief.

When I busted into Papp's trailer there was the other one, that Darlene. I tell you honestly I don't know what all popped into my head. I thought the end of the world had come upon us and everybody was nuts. I got the gun from Papp and I remember I *ran* back to our trailer. I don't run if I can help it because

it is hard on my heart but that time I didn't stop to think I just ran. People was milling around and I had to push my way past them. I guess it did look funny, a big fat woman waving a pistol and trying to run. Not the kind of a thing you would soon forget. I wasn't surprised when they testified how I looked and acted.

When I got inside again everything just stopped dead. Like it was a photograph instead of something happening. There she was with her hair all cut off, standing with all that hair around her feet. She had his straight razor in her hand. I knew she was going to kill him. I could tell by her eyes and I could tell he didn't know it either. The only thing I could do was start shooting.

I must have accidentally hit him first because he looked hurt and fell down by the bunk. Then she came at me with the razor and I didn't see him grab her pistol. I was pointing at her and pulling the trigger but she was not stopping and I realized that my pistol was just going click click. And then there was the noise again only it was her pistol this time and she got hit in the back and fell out flat right in front of me. I saw her eyes go dead before she hit the floor and I looked from her to him and saw his eyes going too and then he fell off of the bunk.

Papp come in and snatched his gun back from me. And right behind him come the police.

It all happened fast and the way I told it and nobody said one word until the police. Not a word, that was the weird part.

I still do not understand. I know I was not shooting to hurt David. That was an accident. And something else I'm pretty sure of now. It was an accident when he shot the girl. He intended to hit me but he wasn't too steady because he was already nigh dead and the girl stepped into the line of fire. The only thing he could have thought was I was out of my mind, gone beserk over jealousy. I will admit I have as much weakness for jealousy as the next woman. I know that's what he thought and he thought I shot him on purpose and he died thinking it. I am sorry I never had a chance to explain.

I am sorry he is dead and I am sorry about the girl too. And I am sorry for Billy Papp because he didn't have anything to do with any of it. I believe, knowing him as I do, he probably was going to steal the money, but I believe he doesn't have sense enough to have done it. Anyway there is no proof we had all that money in the first place. Only the girl's money in the trailer.

Your honor, I know I am guilty of something, but I am not guilty of the thing they have said. It is not true that me and Billy Papp conspired together to rob that girl and David and kill them. I know how it looks. But I also know how it was because I was there.

I have no complaints against anyone. It's a wonder they didn't just lynch the both of us.

I ask you for mercy because I am afraid to die.

If you will let me live I will be grateful in my heart.

But if you cannot find a reason I will not blame you. I cannot promise to be brave, but I will die the best I can. And I believe and trust that Almighty God who has given us so much to bear will be kind to me. I will shed my flesh and weary bones like a suit of old clothes and my heart will be light again. I will be light enough to float on air. I know that once the world is gone and life is gone it will be like when you have had a pain and then the pain is gone. And you can't remember it and it doesn't even matter anymore.

You can see how trusting I am. I do not believe there is a hell anywhere.

I am sorry about causing all the trouble with the electric chair.

There is some trouble I *do* want to cause. I have a sister in San Antonio, Texas, married to a chiropractor named Weatherby. I put her through school and everything, but she has always been ashamed of me and has never done anything for me. When I die and am through with my body you can put it in a box and ship it to her collect. That will give her a chance to make up for what she has done. Don't we all need a chance? And maybe it will end up being a joke on somebody else.

Yours sincerely,
Geneva Frond

The Fiction of George Garrett

WILLIAM ROBINSON

In his recently published third novel George Garrett has his major character remark that man is given "knowledge that the only certainty is perpetual uncertainty; knowledge that the only thing unchanging, changeless, is change itself." These are not new insights, nor even newly rediscovered ones either for a modern or Southern writer. Faulkner for one affirmed their truth in both his fiction and his replies to questions about it. George Garrett might have learned them from Faulkner, with whose work he is intimately acquainted, but he didn't have to, and it doesn't matter, for in the 20th century, an era intellectually dominated by the ideas of evolution, relativity physics, and historicism, change and uncertainty have unchallengable status as ultimate truths, so that when Garrett constructs upon them his latest novel, and by association all his fiction, he profoundly connects it with the vital center of contemporary thought and art.

For a full appreciation of the significance of this connection it must be remembered that the revival of Southern literature in the 30's, and its subsequent position of dominance in American literature, arose from precisely such a connection. When the contemporary imagination became obsessed with time and history, the Southern writer, whose experience with both is rich and deep, could speak not only for his region but for all contemporary men, not only for the disintegration of his traditions but for the decline of Western civilization in general. The Southern writer was no longer a provincial but was qualified as no other American to explore the human meaning of a world under the dominance of change.

Garrett capitalizes upon his advantage as a Southern writer by committing himself as few others have to the South as the origin, subject, and context of his fiction. This commitment comes out in his defense of Faulkner for staying at home in body and spirit to win his art from his native traditions and immediate social circumstances and his attack on the fugitives who have fled to other lands, imaginative or physical, for their success and safety. It is also explicitly present in his first novel, *The Finished Man*, where the protagonist, an expatriate Southerner, returns home to mature by learning to come morally to grips with the community which gave his consciousness finite shape.

But the most important aspect of this commitment is a different and tougher attitude toward change than that taken by the previous generation of Southern writers and the younger ones who have followed their lead. Viewing change from above, from the perspective of a heroic past, they have been so repelled by what they saw happening before them that they could only react to the disintegration of the old order with nostalgia or despair, or at best with irony, another expression of alienation and disengagement. Garrett eludes their sentimentality by viewing change, or the energy which makes it possible, as latent with possibilities as well as threats, at the moment when it breaks through into the world, consciousness, or art.

Garrett's fiction clearly is not an elegy for a dying society or for time-weary man but a vigorous voice of the New South in the making. Energy sweeps through its intense or grotesque characters who are or become involved in the rough give and take demanded by assertive living and its direct, lucid, masculine style, especially effective in the Southern vernacular dialect, a vehicle for the raw power of life. The energy is present also in the rush of action and fury of emotion, impelled by passion and culminating in violence, which characterize his narrative technique, and in experiments with point of view, tense, character types, and plots—resulting from Garrett's persistent quest to tell the true story about change.

Where some others have reacted to the downward tumult of history by espousing symbolism and myth to secure life and art from the terrors of time, Garrett makes truth about change as it is happening, the full complexities of man's life while in the act of living it in and for the present, the sufficient condition of life and art. To say that is not to say that his fiction is rudely realistic or a simple celebration of energy and change. Despair is not replaced by elation or visonary idealism. As naked energy must be disciplined by art to become a significant story, so in life it must be disciplined by responsibility to become humanly valuable. Garrett's favorite story is an account of moral change, a fall from innocence into knowledge, begotten by a violence without evoking a violence within, of involvement in a power struggle from which there is no intellectual or moral escape. To be man, his fiction implies, is to be finite and "guilty"; it is to be a part of the world and responsible to it; it is to live in isolated individuality and with uncertainty and change as absolutes yet care, as Garrett does so obviously for all his fallen characters.

Though change is of the essence, radical change never occurs in Garrett's fiction: man never becomes something more than man, is never reborn into a transcendent state nor allowed to diminish into a mechanism. He is doomed to be himself, simultaneously free and responsible, empowered but moral. This is evident in finished men, who recognize their humanity and are thereby "beholden," and negatively in innocents like Ike Toombs, of "Cold Ground Was My Bed Last Night," who is unrelated and irresponsible. It is true of Red Smalley, a revivalist preacher in *Do, Lord, Remember Me*, who seeks to be free of God's claim upon him as a vehicle of the Word, and Alpha Burns, a fanatical visionary in "To Whom Shall I Call Now in My Hour of Need?" who seeks superhuman power to transform and renew the world. And it is of especial import that the "last" speaker in both stories is the most human of the characters in them. But most definitive is the Wounded Soldier, protagonist in a story of the same name, who is able to be happy during that part of his life when voluntary display of his deformity allows him to be himself, free of pretense or illusion.

Garrett's fiction, then, speaks for a hard-nosed moral realism which, like the Wounded Soldier, achieves its happiness as art by exposing and accepting "a less exalted view of man." Its roots are in are Augustinian doctrine of natural depravity and in the theory and practice of the tale by Poe, who regarded that genre as devoted to accounting for the discovery by reason and conscience of man's worldly and moral identity through close scrutiny of violence or crimes committed in the soul's search for freedom. But its relevance for the present lies in the courage and truthfulness with which Garrett exploits his regional background, particularly the Southerner's sense of man as preeminently social as well as his experience with time and history, to probe into what most absorbs the Western heart and mind today—man's relation to man and the world, expressed sometimes in notions of interrelatedness, I and Thou, dialogue, etc. By involving his imagination in the South to the extent that he does, Garrett illuminates the immediacy of human involvement in general today with vividness and universality. As a consequence, for insight into man as a finite creature in time and this world, and into proper valuing and affirmation of a human life and art, there is no clearer or saner vision than that provided by the fiction of George Garrett.

KEY TO THE CITY

DIANE OLIVER

"Nora, want to eat your breakfast with me?" Her mother's starched uniform swished as she walked to the door.

"All right, Mama, I'm getting up now." She watched her mother push aside the curtain that separated her bedroom from the hallway. Then she swung both feet to the edge of the bed and stood up. The little girl who slept beside her did not stir as Nora pulled on her blue jeans and tiptoed from the room.

In the kitchen her mother already sat at the table. "Babycake still asleep?" she asked. "That child ought to be completely worn out getting ready for this trip. You'd think we'd been to Chicago and back."

Nora slipped her egg from the skillet to the plate. "At least Mattie isn't so much trouble," she said, "but the two of them sure don't help my packing."

"I wish I could help, but Mrs. Anderson is not going to let me off early."

"She still mad about you leaving?"

Her mother nodded and Nora watched the wrinkles around her mouth deepen into soft brown folds. "Time for me to be leaving," she looked at the battered alarm clock on the center of the table. "Listen honey, be sure and get the eggs before the girls get up. The chickens deserve a little bit of peace." She picked up her handbag from the kitchen chair and walked out the door.

Nora rinsed her plate in the kitchen sink, and taking the wicker basket from on top the ice box, opened the screen door. Immediately the hens scurried around her, giggling with cackles as they flapped across the front yard. She looked down at the basket in her hand. Here she was gathering eggs like she did every day of her life and tomorrow the family was leaving for Chicago.

Her daddy had a good part-time job, he said, but he'd gotten so busy he no longer had time to write, not even to send a card for her graduation. She felt strange knowing she would see him in a few hours. Tomorrow morning she and Mattie and Mama and Babycake planned to ride all the way from Still Creek to Chicago without ever leaving the bus except when they all had to go to the bathroom.

Mama probably would have a time with Babycake. Her little sister got sick whenever she rode for a long time, and they couldn't wash her very well in those bus station bathrooms. She knew her daddy would meet them at the downtown Chicago bus station; he would be awfully glad to see them. A lot of people around Still Creek said he'd left them and wasn't going to send for them or even see them again. She had known better. If he said he would send for his family, he would. Besides, when he first married her mama, he promised they'd get away to Chicago. Which was really why Mama took on another job instead of staying home with the kids. With both of them working full time, she figured she could save some money.

At their graduation exercises, the principal had announced the two members of the class who would go on to college. Nora's going to college was the reason they were moving. Her parents said she could go to a branch of the city college practically free and finish up her education. They had planned to move "one of these days" for as long as she could remember.

Nora could repeat their special family formula backwards, frontwards, and even sideways. They had talked about it ever since she was a little girl. Mama and Daddy would get jobs up North, and with the money she herself could earn, she would eventually get through college. Then she would put Mattie through, and Mattie would see that Babycake graduated. And of course if any other sisters or brothers came along, they would do the same thing for them.

She waved to Mrs. McAuley, who was hanging out clothes next door. Her wash, like their family's, was conspicuous with the absence of a man's blue work shirts. Nora wondered if Mr. McAuley would ever come home, but the neighborhood's early morning sounds blotted out the memory of him. Behind the chicken coop she could hear the grinding noise of Mr. Johnson's tractor. How funny to think that in a few hours she would no longer hear that familiar sound. Leaving was just a day away and even thinking about it made her throat feel a little funny.

By the time the eggs were gathered and set up high on top of the ice box, Mama had long since been off to work. Nora made Mattie and Babycake mayonnaise and egg sandwiches for breakfast. After they were through eating, she tried to persuade the two little girls to play house outside. But in an hour they were tired and wanted to help her.

"Go on, Mattie, go back outdoors and play." She tried to keep her impatience from showing.

"But we don't got nothing to play with," Mattie said, determined not to leave. "Margie and Tanker-Belle are all packed up and you said we won't see them again until we get there."

Mattie's brown eyes began watering as if she were going to cry. Margie and Tanker-Belle were the two dolls of the family. Tanker-Belle had been one of those fancy toaster cover dolls that some well-meaning aunt on Mama's side had sent as a Christmas gift. Which would have been nice, but they didn't have a toaster.

Mattie had practically confiscated the doll and for reasons known only to Mattie had named her Tanker-Belle. She had spent most of her time since Christmas in the Pretend House back of the pecan tree. Tanker-Belle was rather frayed now, after having spent several nights in the rain.

Now Nora explained to the little girls that at last the doll was going to have a nice long rest. She had packed Tanker-Belle immediately after breakfast while Mattie was busy with something else. She was now inside the big roasting pan with the dictionary and the kitchen forks. But Mattie insisted that she knew Tanker-Belle was lonesome inside the turkey pan.

"I'll tell you what, Mattie," Nora said as she tried to comfort the sobbing child. "Look on my dresser and get a nickel out of the blue bag. You go find Babycake and you all walk up to Mr. James' store for a double orange popsicle. Then go play in the Pretend House until lunch time."

"Can I, Nora! Oh, can I?" Mattie's smile stopped the tears running down her cheeks. She raced out of the little hallway jumping over boxes and through the bedroom door for a nickel. In a second she was calling Babycake and the two little girls started up the road.

Five dollars and ninety-five cents worth of graduation money was left. Nora kept a mental record of her savings since June. Her habit of saving was a reaction, she guessed. Her father had all the good intentions in the world but whenever they needed money he never had enough. That was one reason why her mother had taken the responsibility of moving the family.

She stooped down and began cramming some books in another cardboard box, in a hurry to move on to something else. By the time the little girls were finished with the popsicle, it would be time for their naps. Nora tied a string around the box and made a double knot. If she could just have an hour by herself, she could finish the packing.

She had begun scrubbing the kitchen floor when suddenly a noise that sounded like a rock hitting the wire of the chicken coop made her drop the rag and run to the back door.

"Babycake, you and Mattie stop bothering the chickens. We won't get any eggs if you keep on; what's wrong with you all anyway?"

"Babycake wants all the popsicle, Nora. And you gave it to me, didn't you Nora?"

By the time Mattie explained about the popsicle and how Babycake had gotten angry and thrown a rock at the chickens, Babycake was crying. Mattie, upon seeing Babycake's tears, had begun crying herself and Nora stood there, outdone. Here she was faced with two squealing little girls and her with all that work to do.

"I can tell," she said firmly, "that it's time for two naps. Give me the popsicle and you can eat it after you've had a nap." She marched her sisters through the back door, stopped to deposit the ice cream on the kitchen table, and continued toward the bedroom. While she undressed her sisters, the popsicle lay forgotten.

In a quarter of an hour Babycake was asleep. Mattie, who was ready to get up again, decided she was not sleepy and began singing to herself. Nora had to stop packing again and tell her to be quiet. She didn't notice the popsicle until she saw the sticky orange drops on her clean kitchen floor. She wiped off the table and floor and swallowed what was left of the dripping orange popsicle. There was no getting around it, she'd have to spend another nickel for some more ice cream.

Nora worked all evening, sorting clothes, folding linen, and packing kitchen utensils. Finally, the boxes were ready to go.

In the morning the smell of freshly fried chicken lingered throughout the house. The two fryers Mama had killed last night plus the one Mrs. McAuley brought over would last them the time the trip would take. In the bottom of the lunch basket were three sweet potato pies and a brown bag full of the Georgia peaches that grew wild in their back yard.

According to the schedule propped on an empty milk bottle on the kitchen table, in a half-hour everybody would be ready to pile in the Edwards' car for the bus station. The Edwards were going to keep all the house furnishings in their barn until Mama sent for the furniture.

The two big beds already had been dismantled and Mattie's roll-away cot was folded up near the front door. Nora walked from the hall into the living room. The whole house looked so empty, even her father's postcards were missing from the mantel over the fireplace. Suddenly she smiled. All of the furniture was covered with old newspapers their neighbors had saved, and four layers of the *Still Creek Bugle* couldn't possibly revive the sagging sofa cushions.

By seven-thirty Babycake had been freshly washed and ironed for the trip. She was commanded to sit still on the front stoop and announce the Edwards' arrival.

Mattie, who also had been dared to get dirty, kept her company. The two little girls sat on the first step, facing the swing tied to the pine tree. Their sliding feet had trampled the bits of grass growing beneath the rope and scattered in the yard were a few green weeds the chickens had not pecked away.

Babycake reached over and gave the potted Christmas cactus a goodbye pat. The leaves were shiny because she had poured water over them this morning—Mama insisted the plant be clean when Mrs. Edwards carried the pot home.

All at once there was a honk from the horn and a long lanky boy, the oldest of the Edwards boys, was running up the steps.

"Pop says are y'all ready yet?" Without giving them a chance to answer he started piling boxes in the trunk of the car. Babycake and Mattie were so scared they would get dirty and get left they did everything Nora told them to do.

"Mattie, pick up the little shoe box. . . . Babycake, make sure we got the lunch. No, I'll take care of the lunch, you pick up the hat box over there." Their little house had never been so cluttered and then so empty. Come to think of it, their neighborhood seldom had seen such excitement.

Everybody in Still Creek was at the bus station to see the Murrays off. There was no need to ask how they'd gotten there. Those few people who had cars drove down and piled in as many neighbors as they could. Uncle Ben, Aunt Mabel's husband, was one of those who had walked the three quarters of a mile to the bus station. Mabel had caught a ride. Anyway, they were all there, a mass of black humanity overflowing the little waiting room marked "Colored."

In one corner of one-half of Still Creek Bus Terminal, Mattie sat on an upright box as Aunt Mabel gave her pigtails a quick brushing. When she had tied each end with a bright yellow ribbon, Mabel thumped Mattie on the neck and pushed her off the box toward her Mama's voice that attempted to round up the family.

Nora saw Aunt Mabel trying to catch Uncle Ben's eye. Mabel began to speak above the noise in the room.

"Haven't been this many people here since they brought that Jackson boy's body home," she said, "the one who was killed overseas three years ago."

While Uncle Ben and Aunt Mabel discussed the community gatherings at the station during the last five years, Mama was getting ready to buy their tickets. Somebody got up so she could sit down and count out the money for four one-way tickets to Chicago.

Mattie was hanging over her shoulders, wide-eyed. "Mama," she breathed, "are we rich?"

"Hush child, I'm trying to count." When she had counted out the correct amount of money four times, she tied what was left into a handkerchief and put it in the blue denim purse which in turn went into her

genuine imitation leather cowhide bag. Still counting silently, she made her way to the ticket window. When the man had given her the tickets and counted out the change, Nora felt like giving a glorious halleleujah of relief. At times like this she always felt something wrong was going to happen. She could imagine the fare going up and them without enough money, having to go back home.

With Mama talking to Aunt Mabel, Nora slipped out of the side door for a final look at her home town. The Georgia landscape was shallow and dull, and to her eyes that had seen no other part of the country, beautiful. Even this early in the morning a thickness had settled over the countryside, covering everything with a film of fine red dust. She fingered the purse inside her pocket. Six dollars she had now—Mrs. Edwards had given her a dime to buy some candy in case she got hungry on the way.

The sound of voices inside the waiting room reached her ears. She could hear Aunt Mabel crying, louder and louder. The voices seemed to reach out and carry her with them. The bus—the bus must have come. Quickly she shut her purse and ran back toward the waiting room.

Sure enough there was her mother frantically hugging and kissing everybody and thanking them for all the good things they had done for the Murrays. Mattie was pulling Mama's hand and begging her to hurry up before they got left. Seeing Nora, her mother beckoned her to come and get Mattie and Babycake for a final trip to the bathroom.

By the time everybody had been pushed out of the waiting room, the men had most of the luggage stored underneath the bus. Then began the last-minute hugging and kissing and gift-giving all over again. Nora felt a dollar bill pressed into her hand. She couldn't help the tears; Uncle Ben really didn't have any money to spare. She bent over and kissed the old man on his cheek.

The bus driver checked his watch and in a dry, matter-of-fact voice announced that anybody who was leaving with him had better hurry up and get on because he was driving in exactly two shakes. Finally the steel door closed. In the rear of the bus, their noses pressed against the window panes, the four Murrays waved goodbye to friends and neighbors and to Still Creek, Georgia, "the original home of fine Georgia peaches."

After hours of riding, Nora lost track of the towns they passed. Still Creek seemed so far away and the slight jogging of the bus no longer made her head ache. The whole trip had become a kaleidoscope of sounds and colors. The small towns surrounded with ranch style houses and green lawns were loose fragments she counted, like turning storybook pages in her mind.

At the next rest stop, Nora decided to stretch her legs in the bus aisle. Mama herself took the little girls inside for a glass of milk and a trip to the bathroom. When the bus started again, she began telling a fairy tale to Mattie and then suddenly the accident occurred. Little Babycake had stuffed herself with too much sweet potato custard and she lost all her dinner on the back seat of the bus. They tried to clean up the seat with some old waxed paper, but they couldn't clean and pay attention to Babycake too.

Babycake started crying. Her stomach hurt and she wanted to go home. Mama tried to hush her, but the more she patted, the more Babycake cried. By the time the sourness had spread throughout the bus, Mama sent Nora up to the bus driver to ask him if he would stop and let Babycake get her stomach settled.

Nora stood up and held on to the seats, cautiously walking up the aisle, toward the back of the bus drivers' gray-blue suit. After hours of riding, the jacket still looked freshly pressed, and he didn't even glance up in the mirror as she approached the driver's seat.

"My little sister's sick," she explained. "If she could get some air, my mother said she might feel better." She held on to the pole near the front steps, facing the back of the driver's gray head.

Muttering something unintelligible, he said No. He had lost enough time and would be stopping soon anyway. They would just have to wait like everybody else.

While she was standing in the aisle, the bus picked up speed and turned a sharp curve. Nora felt herself fall against two elderly women and although the bus was airconditioned, one was struggling trying to raise the window.

"Niggers," she whispered, her voice grating, colliding with the growl of the motor.

Nora was not certain she had heard the woman speak, but even thinking of the word hurt her ears. Nobody'd ever called her a nigger to her face before. At least never with such anger. She looked into the woman's eyes, seeing the fierce look her father often described as belonging to white people. Fierceness that was hatred. She was conscious of the bus moving, jerking to a stop and then moving again but she heard nothing except the woman's words. It was as if the words formed an invisible cloak and only by pushing it away with her thoughts did she keep from being smothered.

She wanted to see her father now—have him take his wife and children from this horrible bus and put them down where they did not have to move ever again. What if . . . No, he would not do that, not after he talked so badly about Mr. McAuley deserting his family six months after they met him in Chicago. The McAuleys stayed in the city not even a year; in December they had come home. Even with the extra money allotted them because of Mr. McAuley's disappearance they did not have enough money to eat. She dared not even think.

Nora never knew how many rest stops the bus made.

Once as she turned toward the window she realized the daylight had changed into darkness. She even forgot to watch for the sign telling them they had crossed the Illinois state line. Mattie wanted to play Cookie Jar, but she could not concentrate on the hand clapping for trying not to remember those words. Nora was almost asleep when the bus turned into an entrance, pulled up to the curb, and stopped.

Because there were so many bundles to carry out, they were the last people getting off the bus. Babycake was the first one to see him. She caught hold of Mama's hand yelling "Here we are, here we are," and started to run across the terminal to the man in the black trenchcoat. Nora had to hold her back. The man Babycake saw was not their father. He was a little too tall, and when he passed the family, he just looked at them strangely.

They stood outside the big glass door with the little packages, waiting and looking through each crowd of people, but no one came.

"You people need help or something?" a woman asked. She walked as if she knew every inch of the ground surrounding the terminal. "If you need a taxi, I'll show you where to stand."

Nora shook her head. "No thank you, we're waiting for someone." Her eyes dropped to the pavement and for a while she was conscious only of shoes, so many different colors, passing, all walking by them. After fifteen minutes and two "May I help you's" Mama guided them through the revolving door and to a bench in the middle of the station.

"That way he can see us when he comes," she said, sitting down on the bench. Nora again braided Mattie and Babycake's hair and then there was nothing to do but wait.

Oh, why hadn't he come. He was supposed to be here, they had sent the letter last Friday. She had told him the exact time of their arrival. Twice she'd written it out.

Now Babycake was getting sleepy again. "Where's Daddy?" she asked, "Aren't we there now?"

"Hush up." Her mother motioned for Nora to unlace Babycake's shoes. "Maybe he can't find us," she whispered above the little girls' heads.

An hour passed. Nora stood. "Where you going?" Mattie asked. "Don't you get lost from us too."

"To check the luggage, it won't take long." Nora began walking down the side of the terminal, near the shiny cigarette machine and past the magazine rack. Everything glittered with a metallic glow but the fluorescent lighting only emphasized the emptiness within her. She looked up and saw an overhead panel advertising a course in shorthand—gt-gd-jb. . . . Then she met Elizabeth Taylor's gaze beneath the sign pointing to the telephone booth.

At once she was aware of what had happened. He was working overtime, and had overslept. She had the apartment building's telephone number from one of his first letters. She would call and whoever answered would tell her where to reach him and then he would come get them. With sticky fingers she loosened a dime from her money collection and lifted the receiver. The phone rang once, and a voice answered:

"McConnell's Drug Store—Hello? This is McConnell's Drug Store."

"Please," Nora whispered, "could I speak with Mr. Joseph Murray."

"Sorry Miss, but no Joe Murray works here."

"Are you sure, don't you know him?"

"No, Lady, but if you want to wait I'll check the list of people working in the building."

Then he was back too soon, and he was sorry, no Murray was even listed there.

Nora emerged from the booth and stood at the lockers, wondering if she should look outside, when she felt someone bump into her. She turned quickly, into a woman tugging on a small boy. "Excuse me," the woman murmured, pushing the boy ahead of her.

Abruptly pulling away, Nora ran toward the doors out to the sidewalk into the darkness. She tried to brush the air from her face but the fingers slightly touching her eyelashes came away damp. She stood outside, her eyes tightly closed, trying not to see them, all three of them huddled on that bench. Then her cheeks were dry.

Nora went back to the station bench and whispered to her mother who was sitting quietly, Babycake's head nestled in her lap.

"Mama? Oh, Mama, did you know all the time?"

Her mother shook her head and reached for her daughter's hand.

"I couldn't know for sure," she said. "We had to work toward something. Don't you see? We wouldn't have ever gotten out if we didn't work toward something." Her voice was sad and quiet, as if she might slowly start humming Babycake to sleep.

"What are we going to do, Mama? They're bound to make us move out of here sometimes."

"We'll just stay right in this spot," she said, covering Babycake with a coat, "just in case." She turned her face toward the suitcases and Nora, seeing that her mother might cry, was sorry she had asked.

"Tomorrow we can call the Welfare people. Somebody there can help us find a place to go." Her mother spoke with her eyes fixed on the travel posters on the far side of the room.

That they never before had had to ask for help made no difference to Nora. She felt that they were pieces in a giant jig-saw puzzle, oddly shaped blobs that would never be put together. Here was her mother sitting so quietly, not letting anything upset her. But then that was not so difficult to do, she herself was not conscious of feeling anything. He loved them, he had to. After all, they were his, but sometimes loving became a burden. And if he had met them at the bus station, perhaps they would have become that to him. But they were supposed to be a family, weren't they? She was no longer certain.

Stepping over the suitcases piled near the bench holding Babycake, Nora began sorting bundles. She looked at the clock on the terminal wall, the silvery hands seemed fixed. Strange that it was morning already, outside the sky was still dark.

She'd probably have to babysit for a while, until Mama found a job and a place to leave the little girls during the day. She began fingering the string around the boxes. Today was Saturday and Mattie and Babycake's Sunday dresses would need ironing, but she'd worry about that later. Their hair ribbons did not have to be pressed, if she could ever remember where they were.

Slowly Nora put down the box. Her shoulders slid down the back of the bench. She couldn't press anything, she couldn't even remember where they had packed the iron.

●●●

The Visit

On fire-escape, on boardwalk, and on sand,
I kept a journal, even during winter.
A makeshift child, how should I understand
That all my structured myths would one day
    splinter?

Last night I brought my journal to your attic.
'My prophet bird, your journal is your cage,'
You said. 'It makes you sorcerous, fanatic.
No prophet bird has ever come of age.

'But you, my love, will come of age, tonight.
Come down to Brighton Beach, and let us quarrel,
Then kiss, and play. And nothing will you write,
But throw your book away, lock, stock, and barrel,

'And live, determined as a meteor.
Your myths are in the sea now, far from shore.'

Deborah Eibel

"THE GREAT SOCIETY THEE." A. HILL.

Collection: Winston-Salem Gallery of Fine

PAUL GREEN

MEN UNITED

When I was a boy in school I often heard the phrase "The American Dream." Later on as I grew up I tried to comprehend the meaning of that phrase. And I think I did.

And now these long years afterward I still believe in it. Yes, believe in it more strongly than ever.

I declare there is such a thing as the American dream. I say *is* although there are many pessimists in our land today who say *was*. It still exists. But its brightness of late has faded. The dreamers don't dream as intensely and vividly or work as hard for it as once they did in the days of Washington and Jefferson. Our last great dreamer and worker in the American tradition was Woodrow Wilson with his vision of a world of free men united in common idealism and brotherhood. In some ways Franklin Roosevelt, it seems, tried to follow after him.

And what is this American dream?

In his *The Epic of America* the historian James Truslow Adams several years ago said, "We cannot become a great democracy by giving ourselves up as individuals to selfishness, physical comfort and cheap amusements. The very foundation of the American dream of a better and richer life for all is that all in varying degrees shall be capable of wanting to share in it. If we are to make the dream come true, we must all work together, no longer to build bigger, but to build better. There is a time for quantity and a time for quality. The statistics of size, population and wealth would mean nothing to me unless I could still believe in the dream." So said James Trulow Adams.

These are good words.

What is this American dream?

It is just that. It is a dream—a vision, an ideal of a nation and of a world of other nations in which self-reliant men, men of good will, of dedicated strength of mind and character live and have their cooperative being.

It is a theory and a commonsense philosophy of government which declares in its own ringing terms that each individual has his right of and his responsibility to the fullest self-development of his talents as becomes the dignity and worth of a man.

It is a dream then, an ideal of self-government, of liberty in that government and responsibility co-equal with that liberty.

In short it is a religious dream. And truly it is sound social science as well. And its configuration and essential statement were laid down long ago in Greek thought and in the New Testament and in the teachings of a young carpenter named Jesus Christ who later becam a man-crowned divinity and so was burdened forevermore with the title the Lord.

It was also stated and written down half a millenium before that by another great spirit and soul Buddha, the Lord in Asia.

And by Confucius in China and more lately by Mahatma Gandhi in India. And before him by Leo Tolstoy in Russia.

It is a dream that has existed in the breasts of all good and just-acting and right-thinking men of every age and condition and law.

Today the dream is being challenged, is being threatened, both at home and elsewhere, and if it is to continue to flourish on this earth and grow green with the hopes of aspiring men everywhere of whatever clime, period or condition, color or creed, then each of us must become conscious of our need and our duty. We must get busy now as never before in the cause of well-doing and service to it.

For a crisis of world tragedy and advancing horror looms above us all.

There must be no weakening, no yielding, no lying down before this monstrous barbarity of blind power which threatens us so direfully with its reach and ruin.

And what is this barbarity? It is hate and fear, and fear and hate—all personified in the doctrine of perverted and one-sided nationalism.

II

Not too long ago I completed a trip of several months into many nations of Asia and Europe, including Russia. And I had the privilege once more of looking at my own homeland through the eyes of other people and of hearing her interpreted by alien critics on alien soil.

And neither by my own thought and words nor by the thought and words of others could I be happy about my country.

Confusion and frustration thus are among us. And each day these vices would seem to increase, whipped into more frenzy and fervor by the very agencies which should seek to allay them and steady us in our moral purpose and solid social intent.

The American dream as it was visioned forth by Washington, by Jefferson, by Abraham Lincoln and Woodrow Wilson struck the heartstrings of the world in a great chord of harmony and friendship and admiration.

But these leaders are gone. Who has risen in their stead?

And daily we are losing more support and more friends in this wide world.

Not so long ago then the friendship of most of that world was ours. But today it is no longer true.

As the presidential candidate Wendell Willkie once said, there was a great reservoir of friendship existing for us in the world. Today it is sadly diminished and is growing less each succeeding day.

A young newspaper reporter in Singapore for instance said caustically to me at the opening of our interview—"what does America intend?"

I could not answer him that it was—power. I was ashamed to.

That question is still being asked by millions of people in Asia and parts of Europe and South America as they turn discouragedly toward other allies and another ideology. For our actions are giving the answer.

The people of the world are confused by our confusion, frustrated by our frustration and infected with the fear which is our fear—a fear which strangely and viciously enough now has become a fear mainly of us —us now the potential enemy and no longer the friend of mankind.

For generations the majority of the Asiatic people, for instance, were friends of the American people. They were inclined to work with us toward a united world and a better day for man everywhere. For we had the physical power as well as the ideals for such leading, and until recently, I say, they have had the will and the urge to go with us.

But now in these latter days they feel that our ideals are falling behind our physical power, a power too often used too recklessly. We are strong in the arm, but lacking rightness in the heart and clarity and logic of ideals in the head. The American dream is being betrayed.

So they feel.

Indeed they look upon our present foreign policy, like some of us at home, with incredulity and dismay. They see a most powerful physical nation almost bankrupt and undone as to creative international thinking and dynamic policies for the healthful development of the world. They see a mighty nation run ragged at home by civil disobedience, violence and crime and cheap sensationalism—a nation which in its hysteria of self-failure and error identifies any and every kind of tyranny or error with communism and sees in every dark shadowy place of hill and dale some subversive

agent or influence inimical to its safety and its soul.

They see a hundred and eighty million people burdened with a terrific taxation—of whose every dollar sixty cents goes wastefully and grotesquely to pile up atom and hydrogen bombs, aircraft, guns, tanks, rockets, missiles and create the galling harness of iron-footed war. (Already we along with Russia have enough bombs to destroy the total living world.)

They see a giant of a nation with a great gun in his hand. And the heavier the gun the greater the giant's irresponsibility and fear. It would seem he has got himself locoed—haunted, bewitched as it were, in short bogged down in a neurosis of materialism.

So they think.

And Asia and much of Europe and the South below us, as I say, are becoming more suspicious and afraid of us than ever before. And we must remember there are some two billion people who are thus becoming suspicious and fearful.

In Malaya I saw it true. In Indonesia, in Thailand, in Burma, Japan and in India, in Pakistan, and even lately in the Philippines. And it has already for years been true in China. And alas, alas, what of the American terror now let loose in Vietnam—and all in cynical disregard of the United Nations.

III

We are losing friendships every day on other counts too. We are backing the wrong people in too many places. We are giving our strength to effete and oppressive colonialisms, to authoritarian dictators and reactionaries—in Malaya, in Indo-China, in Formosa, Spain, in the Middle East and in the Caribbean and South America too. And all the while the people are crying for freedom, for bread and for a chance to develop their own lives and share in the bountiful goods and glories of this world.

And they are determined to have that chance and so to share. And they will.

The Minister of Education for an eastern country recently spoke the fervor and the faith of the new day when I heard him say—"Asia is on the march. She has waked up. Nothing will stop her in her progress toward a fuller life." Men everywhere then are waking up and are beginning to march.

The Asiatic dream as well as the world dream now is the dream that once we had and for which we fought our own revolution of freedom from tyranny. And it is a dream we must share in again, must help to make live more strongly again. Or we shall fall further out of step with the march of the hundreds of millions in the world, shall be further isolated and left finally alone in misery and second-rateness in our own graveyard of rusting military might.

And woe on woe, for out of that graveyard will arise the screaming demon of wrath and blood and fire—this of our own creating.

"D-40-65"   MACKEY

THE SUMMER OF THE WHITE COLLIE

CHARLES EAST

FOR BLANCHE

That summer I was twelve my grandfather came to live with us and he brought his white collie, old Lou. She was a funny kind of dog; she never had much to do with me. She never had much to do with anybody, except the old man. She was his dog. He'd lie there sick in bed, in the back room, and she'd lie there by the armoire close to him. At night my mother'd let her out. Before long she'd be at the door, to be let in: you could almost set the clock by her. But one night she didn't come to the door, and the next morning my father found her. She had been shot. One of the farmers down the road had shot her; he thought she was a wolf. And everybody was worried about telling

the old man that somebody had shot his dog.

That was the first I knew. I mean, about him, how sick he was and all. My father had gone down in the pasture to bury old Lou. He came across the yard, wet from the rain, and my mother met him at the steps. "How're we gonna tell Papa somebody shot his dog?" He had had old Lou since I could remember. He and old Lou had lived in that big house with the latticed porches and the lightning rods.

"We're not goin to," my father said.

My mother looked at him. "What you mean?" she said.

"It's no use to."

"What're we gonna tell him, then?"

"Oh," he said, "she run off. Lit out for home. When she was young she coulda made it, but she was old . . ."

"You think . . . ?"

"A dog'll do that."

"I know," she said, "but . . ." You could tell by her voice it bothered her. "You think we'd be doin the right thing? I mean, to keep it from him?"

My father smiled. "As old as your papa is," he said, "as old and as sick as he is, you know what he'd do?" A roll of thunder shook the house. "He'd get up from there and he'd go lookin for whoever shot that dog."

There was a quiet: the rain had stopped. Then I heard my mother say, "You think Papa *knows*?" I thought she meant about old Lou.

My father shook his head. "He thinks he's gonna get up from there "

"Sometimes," she said, "I have the feeling Papa *knows*."

That was when I knew—that they'd brought my grandfather here to die with us, that he'd die not knowing old Lou had died, too. It bothered me. I guess because I'd never known anybody who was going to die before. I wanted to say something—I don't know what. Maybe ask my mother why, and what it was like, as if she knew. I guess when you know, it's too late, and nobody asks you, and if they did you wouldn't tell them anyway.

She was no good at pretending. My mother, I mean. But all that week she was on the phone, calling the people out there where papa used to live, asking them, "Have you seen old Lou? Has old Lou showed up yet?" And all that week my grandfather was lying there in bed in the next room, listening to that phoning she did because she didn't want him to know his dog was dead. Every once in a while she'd go out on the gallery and call, and then she'd come back in and say, "No sign of her yet, Papa."

He'd turn and look at her.

She'd try to make him talk. "Papa," she'd say, "how long have you had old Lou?"

He'd think a while. "Now," he'd say, "you're asking me . . ."

"I know about the time this child was born."

He'd think some more. "Along about . . ."

"Thirty-seven."

"That's right," he said. "Thirty-seven."

"Well," she said, "if somethin's happened to her . . . I hope nothin's happened to her, but if somethin has . . ." She kind of laughed. "You know what you used to tell me: a dog is a dog, there's always another dog where that one come from."

For a minute he didn't say anything, as if he didn't hear. Then he said, "Ella B. . . ." B. was for Beatrice, my mother's middle name. "Ella B., I had lotsa dogs. Coon dogs. Bird dogs. But wasn't none of em smart like old Lou."

My mother smiled at that. "Well, we're gonna get you another dog," she said. "You hear that, Papa? And when you get on your feet again, you'll have a dog you can take back home with you."

That summer I thought about it. It bothered me, knowing my grandfather was going to die and didn't know about it, didn't know about old Lou. I'd go out to the barn and I'd climb up in the loft and sit there, wondering. What was it like to die? What was the mystery? I did a lot of thinking, and one evening about suppertime I went in the old man's room. He was asleep. At least, I thought he was. His eyes were shut. When they were open they were watering. Then he moved his head and I saw that he wasn't asleep, just lying there the way old people do.

"Hi, boy," he said.

"How you feel, Grandfather?" I said. I said it loud. I always spoke loud to him.

"Oh . . ." he said. He didn't say how he was feeling. Maybe he didn't know how he was feeling. "What time is it, boy?" he said.

And I said, "Suppertime." I guess that wasn't what he meant. I guess when you've lived eighty years you don't care whether it's suppertime or dinnertime. But I said, "Suppertime."

And he said, "Lean down, boy."

I leaned down.

"Old Lou . . ." he said, "old Lou's dead, ain't she?"

I just looked at him. And then I said it. I hadn't meant to, but there I was, looking down at him, and the room was dark and there were fireflies at the windowscreens. "Grandfather," I said, "old Lou didn't run off. One of the farmers shot her. Down the road. He thought she was a wolf."

The old man just laid there. He didn't get mad. He didn't get up from there like my father said he would and go after the farmer down the road. He just laid there.

I was almost to the door when I heard him calling me. "Boy . . ." he said.

I walked back to the bed.

"You're not . . ." He swallowed and coughed. "You're not gonna tell your mama you told me, are you?"

I shook my head.

"That's good," he said. For a minute I stood there. Then I heard her and he heard her: my mother calling me. "Run to supper, boy," he said.

I ran to supper, but I couldn't eat. I went to my room, laid there, wondering. And then it all made sense—the old man and the collie dog, the summer, all of it. Late one afternoon that summer he died. My mother sat there by his bed, rocking, fanning, watching the pulse beat in his arm. To the last they pretended. "Papa," she said, "now as soon as you get up from here, we're gonna get you another dog you can take back home with you."

"I can take back home with me," he said.

GATEWOOD

THE FIGHTING COCKS

HARRIET DOAR

Sitting on the back steps, snapping beans into a crockery bowl, Ellie Mae looked thoughtfully at the brilliant birds in the pen. The pen itself, stilted to keep the feet of royalty off the ground, was knocked together from old gray boards and chicken-mesh. In the dull frame the ruffled black and red feathers, polished by the sun, glowed with life and color until they seemed about to explode into flame. The reptilian claws moved delicately now without the steel that turned them into raking death.

Ellie Mae frowned. "Devils," she said. They craned their necks and glared fiercely back at her, one of them whirring its burnished wings against the wire. That's what they were, too, red and black devils. Pleased with herself, she smiled into the sun.

Ellie Mae looked up and down the row of yards, all alike as the inch-lengths of green beans falling into the bowl. The afternoon was windless and warm, so warm that the old blue sweater around her shoulders was a little more than she needed. But it wasn't spring yet, only a brief warm winter day, and the buds were still tightly clenched on the trees. There was no green out except the shoots in the onion beds, and the ground was littered with the dry reminders of last summer's grass. In the railroad cut, scabrous vines clung to the red earth like lichen shrinking into itself. The little yards were all saggingly fenced in as a token of privacy, each with its ridiculous outhouse like something a child would draw, and sprawling down the hill beyond the fences were the jagged bars of pigpens. Of all the lots on the Hill, theirs was the only one that was different. The gray pen stood out in the yard, holding its two jeweled creatures up for every one to see.

The sun was right in her eyes now; Ed would be home any time. Ellie Mae moved clumsily to get up, dusting off the seat of her skirt. She looked across the gash made by the railroad, into the fields beyond, edging off into woods.

"Johnny . . ." she screamed. "Mae Belle . . ." There was no answer. I'm gonna wear them two out one of these days, she promised herself. I told 'em not to get outa hearin' distance.

After she put the beans on, she splashed cold water on her face and made it up carefully in front of the kitchen mirror, dampening her hair a little and crumpling it in her hands to push the curl in. From the top drawer, where it lay coiled among the knives and spoons, she took a piece of blue ribbon and tied it around her head, subduing the thick dark hair that hung below her shoulders. This was her private ritual; she wasn't going to look like the rest of the women on the Hill when they got a family. Even when she was worn out and didn't feel good, she made the extra effort; she always wanted to look a little better for Ed. Now that she was in the family way again, she'd be that much more careful. The skirt stretched tight across her stomach and hiked up in front; she'd need a new dress before long. She stood a moment with her hands resting on the gentle curve, lost in an ancient timeless contemplation.

The sweet, salty odor of fatback filled the kitchen as the beans cooked. Standing at the sink, Ellie Mae heard the familiar straining rattle before she saw Ed's car come over the rise. He stopped to let Louie out next door, and Louie lingered a while talking, as if he hated to go into the house. Louie looked tired and slack, standing on the unpaved walkway, all one color, a kind of all-over tan that blended into the dirt, as if he didn't want anybody to notice him. His shoulders, warped by years of doffing, drooped more than usual; his eyes were squinched from watching the whirling spindles endlessly fatten. Watching them, she saw the kids come running up and tumble clamoring into the car. I believe they can smell him coming, she thought; they're like puppydogs. They always managed to turn up from nowhere just as he got home.

Ed was whistling as he walked by the window, the kids clinging to him and talking up at him. He always came in the back way to take a look at the birds. With the bent figure of Louie still in her mind, she looked at Ed with pride. He didn't seem any older, she thought, than the day they were married, not like a settled married man with two children and another one on the way. No, he was young and unbroken; would he ever really settle down? His step was light and springy; she'd like to go dancing one more time before she got too big . . . maybe she'd leave the children over at her sister's one night. The dark blue work pants swung low on his waist, tight to the narrow, hard hips. His dark skin looked warm and lively against the blue shirt. His straight black hair had an inky sheen to it; sometimes when he was drinking he said he had Indian blood in his family, and then when he was sober he said no, he hadn't, he was only fooling. She didn't know for sure; she believed him whichever he said. Anyway, there was something wild about him; you never did know just what he was thinking.

He had an old jacket swung over his shoulder, and as he came in he threw it on a chair and crossed over and put his arm around Ellie Mae. The warm touch soothed and quickened her at the same time; she picked up the spoon to stir the beans again, feeling happy.

"I won't be here for supper," he said.

She turned to look at him.

"I got to be down the road by dark."

All she said was, "You be back tonight?"

"Might be. Might be tomorrow or tomorrow night." He leaned against the doorframe. "No hurry." His eyes were watching her. "Los' my job today, Ellie. Quit or got fahred. It was a draw."

She sighed and turned back to the sink. "I'll go down tomorrow and see can I get some spare work," she said, when the silence had stretched out too long and tight. "Wash your hands, Johnny, you too, Mae. You know you can't come to the table thataway."

The two children dipped their hands in running water, keeping their round-eyed gaze on their father, splashing water on their fronts.

"You goin' somewhere? Kin I go too?" It was the boy's young husky voice, but the girl's face asked too.

"No, you can't," Ellie Mae said sharply. She felt Ed's eyes on her, but she didn't look up.

He put a folded wad of bills on the table, sliding it under the edge of the coffee pot. "I'll see you," he said as he picked up his jacket.

I didn't need to say it that mean, Ellie Mae thought. He wasn't fixin' to take the kids anyway. She watched from the back porch as he coaxed the cocks into their small traveling cages. He held each one a moment, examining it, smoothing it down, testing the springy muscles. The children stood at a cautious distance; they knew the power of the proud beak, its lightning dart. Ellie Mae was afraid of the cocks herself. Well, not exactly afraid; it wasn't that they'd hurt her—although she was careful not to get too close—but they made her uneasy. There was something wild about them, something opposed to houses and backyards, clothes on the line, supper smells from the kitchen. Something alien, threatening, like the wicked gleam of yellow in the arrogant eyes.

She was afraid of them, but he was the boss, hard as they, as dark, compact, and sure. There was a kind of link there that drew them together and shut the family away; she guessed that was why she fussed about the cocks and the time Ed spent with them, coaxing, bullying them into resiliency, feeding them, watching them, nursing them back to health when they came home wounded from battle, their eyes proud and wicked as ever for all their limp, bloody feathers.

It was lonesome without Ed. She wondered a little resentfully about that male world down the road. He could go, but she could just stay here and think: think about what they needed and where the money would come from. Oh well, something would turn up. Behind her now, in the kitchen, she could hear Mae Belle whining, "Mama, make him quit, mama . . ."

"Can't you leave me alone two minutes, you two?" She turned in exasperation. "Don't give anybody a chance to hear themselves think." She cuffed both of them impartially and competently and began to spoon up the supper.

II

She wasn't really worried about the job, not at first. Ed and the second hand, Squint Pegram, were always quarreling and falling out, and Ed always went back. He was a good fixer, and suppose he did lay off a little every now and then? She didn't start worrying until she'd been working a couple of weeks herself, and Squint had called her out of the noise, out into the harsh sunlight with her ears still ringing, to talk to her. She got two or three days a week, and that was about all she could make anyhow, with the kids and the house, the washing and ironing and all. But working made her hungrier, and it was getting harder to stretch the money. How long could she manage? She had forgotten how tired you could get walking around the frames; she felt slow and clumsy. She was getting bigger, too; she needed that dress. Sometimes she could hear the sound of the frames going on and on in her head long after she was home, and she knotted threads in her sleep.

Squint had been firm. "I've had enough of that fool runnin' around. You got one of the nicest houses on the Hill and only one in the family working. Okay, that's all right, but that one's got to work steady and keep at it. Goen off two-three days at a time; who does he think he is? He could get away with it before when I couldn't hire nobody else and had to put up with it. But I got to have somebody I can depend on, you know that, Ellie, you know I got to have hands I can depend on. He's gonna get in trouble, too, one of these nights—get cut up or shot up or in jail or something. Then where will you be? Now listen, whenever Ed gets ready to come back here and tell me he aint goen off fighten them cocks no more, all right. All right, I don't hold no grudges. Only I can't wait forever."

"Well, you know he aint gonna give up fighten," Ellie had said, a little contemptuously. She'd get mad at Ed for not buckling down, and then she'd look at somebody like Squint, with his tobacco-stained teeth and his sandy eyebrows, his hairy hands and his left eye that bent inward and gave him a funny air of deep study. Maybe she had looked at Squint too long, because then he had started talking about the house again. Just let Ed make up his mind, he said, that was all he asked. She could work on a while, he wanted to do what was fair, but there was a lots of folks would appreciate a house like that right now.

The door banged behind Ellie Mae as she picked up the basket of wet clothes and carried it out back. The weight staggered her, and she felt dizzy when she dropped it to the ground and straightened up again. She reached to steady herself on the pen, and the cock nearest her darted his neck at her snakewise, looking at her with little malevolent, yellow-gleaming eyes. She drew back, and her feelings concentrated on the ruffled brilliance. "I'd like to pull every one of them red feathers out and put you in a stew pot," she muttered. She turned away and began to pin the clothes to the line with vicious jabs.

That night she cried miserably to herself in bed. She hadn't cried since she was a little girl, since she couldn't remember when. The children slept restlessly in the next room, Mae Belle making little whimpering sounds, Johnny still clutching the comic she'd let him buy to shut him up. The other half of the bed was empty; Ed was out somewhere getting drunk, she knew. He had slammed out in the middle of supper—if you could call it supper; she couldn't blame him, now that she had time to think. She never should have talked to him like that.

She sat up in bed and pressed her fingers into her eyes, wiping the tears angrily away. "Them birds mean more to you than your own children," she had said bitterly, vindictively. "*They*'re not hungry." It had been the kids' whining and fussing that had started it

and got on Ed's nerves until he'd lashed out at Johnny. Oh why hadn't she kept her big mouth shut? Well, that wasn't all of it, but that was what stuck tight in her mind. And he was feeling bad enough already; he knew why the kids were whiny. Ed didn't get mad too easy, but when he did it was scary; and he hadn't said anything then, just walked out and slammed the door.

She heard the back door come gently to, heard cautious, unsteady steps; she lay down hastily, turning her back to the emptiness. For a few minutes, when he touched her, she remained rebelliously rigid; her heart was full of meanness she did not herself understand. Then resistance drained away, leaving her soft and defenseless. Even the sandpaper beard and the smell of whisky were comforting.

"Why, you've been crying," he said wonderingly.

She shook her head fiercely, but did not answer. Later, wanting to talk, she began, in the darkness, "Ed . . . Ed?" Raising herself on an elbow, she saw with exasperated tenderness that he was already asleep.

III

"Now scat, both of you," she said. "And you better stay as long as they'll feed you."

She gave Mae Belle a pat on the rump to get her started. "And no fighten, remember?" She stood in the doorway and watched their skinny shapes diminish along the roadway. Mae's rolled-up curls bobbed against her head; where did she get that little sharp-pointed face? But Johnny was the spittin-image of his father, even to the budding swagger of his walk.

She watched them over the rise. She wanted them good and gone before Ed got home. She had slept later than usual, not hearing the ragged chorus of birds at daybreak. Ed had been gone when she waked with the sun on her face, through the east window. The morning was clear, with only a little chill left in the air; she felt fresh and rested. She swept the house out briskly, her mind busy now, and full of purpose.

She hadn't wanted to leave here; it had seemed terrible to get out and leave the place where they'd lived so long. Now she saw, with the dust swept out of her mind, that it was the only thing to do. They could sell the furniture, whatever they could get for it would help. Her sister wouldn't mind too much keeping the kids for a while, she wouldn't hardly notice two more with her brood. She'd been staying away from there since Ed wasn't working, not to get into any arguments; her sister never had taken much to Ed. Well, she'd just tell her she wasn't feeling so good, and then, when they got located again, she'd make it up to her some way. Maybe they'd get into some other kind of work. Maybe farming. That's what Ed had come from, a little farm up in the foothills; that's where he'd learned how to handle the cocks. Well, she'd let him worry about where. Whatever he wanted, that suited her; she was sick of all this fighting and arguing. No sense to it; it was enough to make a man tired of being married at all. There were other places in the world, other jobs, she guessed. Squint could have his old house.

Now that she saw her way clear, now that she'd made up her mind, she felt free of a weight. She sang snatches of old songs as she scrubbed the floors, songs the jukeboxes had been playing when Ed was courting her, and pieces of hymns she remembered hearing her mother sing. She wished Ed would come on back, for she was impatient now to talk; only a small doubt nagged at her. Maybe he would still be mad about what she had said; well, the sooner he came, the sooner she'd know. She pushed the doubts away, impatient with them too.

She was getting restless with nothing to do. And lightheaded, for she had eaten the last of the bread for breakfast. She had thirty-five cents in the kitchen drawer; she would walk over to the store and get what she could. She started out the back way and in the door stopped, her hand on the frame. Automatically, she had looked for the brilliant flash of plumage in the yard. But the pen sagged open; the bright birds were gone. She stood still, looking at the emptiness. Her legs felt weak. She went back to the kitchen and slumped into a chair. She sat a long time without moving.

No use to move now. Now that it's happened, she thought dully. This was what she'd been afraid of all the time, every time she looked at those snaky devils stepping so delicate and proud, watching her with their hateful eyes. Afraid that he'd reach in and take the cocks and be off down the road, off into that strange land of male equality that barred her out, that didn't know she existed, didn't care. A world ringed around the shuffling birds, the flashing claws and feathers, the wicked beak and eye, the slashing, needle-sharp steel: a world where a mill hand, with his own tough veterans, was anybody's match. It wouldn't be hard to forget a house and a mean-tongued wife, a couple of whiny kids.

She got up quickly, took her thirty-five cents and went along to the store. He'd come back. He always came back. He'd only gone for the day or maybe the night. But why had he left so early? He'd never gone off before without telling her. She wouldn't think about it. He'd come back. They'd make out. They always had made out. She wouldn't think about it any more.

She picked up a loaf of bread and a can of pork and beans, looking at the thick slabs of meat and the cheese and bacon. A half a country ham. Chunks of stew beef. Fat pork chops. She could smell them cooking. She could taste them. The dime wouldn't help much anyway—she'd get a candy bar. She'd been craving something sweet and gooey. But while she stood there waiting she saw a new piece of ribbon on the counter, a plaid piece, and when the clerk got around to her, she bought a yard of that instead. For when Ed came home. He had to come home.

But it gave her a real start when she got back and saw the old car out front. She didn't hear any sound and she was almost afraid to look into the kitchen. There he was, though, looking at a cup of coffee in front of him. She was so relieved she couldn't think of a thing to say. She felt weak all over, like the time Mae Belle fell down in the road right smack in front of a car, and she thought sure the man couldn't stop, but he did.

Ed looked up at her dully.

"I got my job back," he said. "Second shift, though. Start back tomorrow."

She smiled, sliding down into a chair on the other side of the table. "I knew Squint'd back down," she said.

"I sold them two birds I had here," he said. "I sold the ones I had out, too, the whole lot. Sold 'em to a feller got more time to fool with 'em. He's been after me. There's the money—most of it, anyway. You can buy something fit to eat for a change." He scowled at the can of pork and beans, keeping his eyes away from hers.

"Sold the birds . . ." she echoed stupidly.

"You heard me, didn you? There wasn't any money left to bet 'em, nohow." He stood up; his hands were thrust hard into his pockets. "I'm tahred . . . I been ridin since before daylight. I'm goen to sleep. Call me when you got supper on the table."

Ellie Mae followed him, after a moment, into the bedroom. There was something she wanted to say, but she couldn't think just what. She looked down at the back of his head, his black lank hair, and finally put a piece of blanket over him, touching his shoulder, but he did not move.

Ellie Mae went out on the back steps and sat down, looking at the empty pens. She still had the money clenched in her hand; it had been cold, now it was warm. It was food, lots of food, and maybe some new clothes, too. Shoes, anyway, for the kids. She should have been happy, but instead she had an odd feeling of hurt inside. And fear. There was no need to be afraid any more, she reminded herself.

She looked off into the clouds gathering for sunset. He had to have a job, didn't he? All those crazy plans of hers—big and clumsy as she was, to go piling off, leaving the kids maybe hungry, maybe sick. She remembered then that she hadn't fixed her face or put on the new ribbon. But it didn't matter. It came to her suddenly how silly it was: a big fat pregnant woman tying a red plaid ribbon around her head, trying to look pretty. It was so silly she didn't know whether to laugh or cry.

The sun was going down beyond the row of back yards, all alike, an even gray; and twilight damp filled the air. It was time to think about supper again.

THE SOUTH, THE LAW, AND ME

KATHRYN

JOHNSON

NOYES

Blessed with the combination of a mild disposition, a cautious nature and good luck, I had lived for thirty-four years without running counter to the law or having anything more serious to do with its officers than requesting directions—until December 28, 1963. On that day, in a restaurant in Chapel Hill, North Carolina, I was arrested and literally carted off to jail. My offense was attempting to order Sunday dinner while in the company of a white friend named William Cash and eleven young Negro students, at an establishment on the outskirts of town called *The Pines*.

We arrived quietly, went into the dining room, and sat down at tables and booths, waiting to be served. This may or may not strike any given individual as a peculiar thing for me to have done, but I will digress for a moment here to explain why I did it: I did it because I live in the state of North Carolina, work here and am raising a family of four children here. I believe that what happens in my state and my country is my business, and I believe that what has been happening in the South for generations is monkey-business of the very first order. I had come to a private confrontation with myself and my beliefs, and the only way I could justify myself or the moral code I have tried to instill in my children was to *act*; to commit an overt deed of my own will and volition. I did not involve myself in the civil rights movement out of pity for the Negro or anyone else. I involved myself because of my personal outrage that *my* state— which I, as a taxpayer, helped to support—was perpetuating a system both morally indefensible and inhumanly cruel. I did it, to put it simply, for purely selfish reasons; me and mine.

The thirteen of us (two of our number young boys under sixteen, Mr. Cash and I in our thirties) sat quietly waiting for a waitress to appear and take our order. Finally the hostess came over to our booth and said, "You'll leave, of course."

"We'd like to see a menu," my friend replied.

The hostess went away. Several reporters from a television station and two newspapers arrived in the parking lot at about this time, and the employees ran through the building locking the doors so that the newsmen could not get in. We waited. After ten or fifteen minutes, three police cars drove up and the officers were admitted to the building. I do not know whether the officers were aware that we had been locked in during the interval. Captain Durham, second-in-command of the Chapel Hill Police Department, walked up to our booth with the manager of the restaurant. Moving from one to another of us, the manager shook his finger in our faces and chanted, "I am the manager and I ask you to leave."

Feeling that we had committed no crime or social indiscretion, we remained as we were. The other officers then entered the dining room and began carrying us out to the waiting cars. As the policemen lugged me past the covey of irate waitresses in the lobby, one of those ladies spat in my face. "Thank God that isn't my daughter!" she said.

We were driven to jail at about seventy miles an hour and booked on two counts; trespassing and resisting arrest. The North Carolina Trespass Law is patently unconstitutional and was designed to prevent people of Negro descent from using public accommodations within the state. As for resisting arrest; nobody seems to be sure even now whether or not passive inactivity is the same thing as resisting. But there we were.

After asking me my name, address, occupation, age and race (I refused to answer this latter question), the policemen took my purse and ushered me into a cell designed for four inmates. Eleven of us spent the night there. After all the bookings had been accomplished, one of the jailers came into our area and I asked him if I might make a telephone call. He replied that I could call a bail-bondsman if I liked, but no one else. I told him that because I believed I had committed no crime, I would not spend money on a bondsman. He walked away. A little later, he came back and I again requested to be allowed to use the phone, to call my home in Durham. The officer was polite, but said no, not unless I would call for bail. I then told him that it was my constitutional right to make one phone call (I had heard this somewhere, but was not at all certain it was true) and he looked confused but finally agreed to usher me upstairs if I would hurry, because the 'Chief' was out and might return at any time. We went to the police offices on the ground floor of the building and I attempted to call my family but couldn't get through. The officer was nervous and kept watching the door, and finally he insisted that I go back to my cell without having contacted anyone.

That night, two of my cellmates left on bail and the rest left the next morning—all excepting a seventeen year old girl named Peggy. Peggy, discovering that I intended to remain in jail until we could be heard in Recorder's Court, elected to stay with me, and I am very glad that she did. If I had been alone, the experience would have been many times worse than it was.

The cell was very cold; there was an ice storm raging outside and the walls and floor of our little basement home were made of cement. On the last day of nineteen sixty-three, which was the most difficult for Peggy and me, the jailer gave us each two cold fried egg sandwiches and a Pepsi-Cola at six a. m. and then disappeared. We did not see another soul until long after it was dark, and for some reason there was no heat turned on that day. Our cell was about fourteen feet long and eight feet wide, barred on two sides with cement walls on the other two. It contained a toilet, a sink with cold water and four bunks along the long wall. Each of the bunks had an army blanket on it and Peggy and I divided them and wrapped ourselves up. The blankets smelled foul, but we were very cold and decided that we would rather risk contracting a rare and obscure disease from the blankets than freeze to death on the spot. The day before, a minister had been allowed to visit us and he had given us some chewing gum. We now held the unwrapped sticks of gum in our fists, next to our noses, and this helped somewhat to disguise the stench of the blankets. We spent the hours singing, telling each other stories, discussing life and trying to keep warm. Peggy was exactly half my age, a chubby, attractive young Negro girl who had been born and raised in Chapel Hill. Despite the obvious differences between us, we discovered that we had many things in common, most notably a highly active sense of humor, and were able to help each other through the day and avoid depression.

At about eight o'clock that night several policemen came downstairs, opening the doors into the corridors and turning on all the lights. One of them said to me, "You're going to have company—your friends are raising hell all over town."

Several of the demonstrators who were arrested that night had attempted to purchase a loaf of bread at a small grocery store called The Rockpile. This store is owned and operated by a man named Carlton Mize. Mr. Mize and his wife do not like Negroes and their store had always displayed a 'White Only' sign, although almost every other store of its kind in the state has always served all customers. The Rockpile was a

logical target for the demonstrators because of this and because Mr. Mize frequently held late-night meetings at his store with carloads of men from the rural areas around Orange County. That night, New Year's Eve, Mr. Mize was visited by a group of young people of both races, and when he would not serve them, they sat down on the floor and sang hymns. Mr. Mize then locked the outside door of his store and went to his shelves for bottles of ammonia, which he poured over the heads and down the backs of the students. Finally, one of them got away and ran outside to call the police from a pay station. The police came and arrested the demonstrators for trespassing. Several weeks after this incident, Mrs. Mize wrote a letter to the *Durham Morning Herald* in which she said that both she and her husband had prayed to God for guidance in these hard times, and that they were convinced in their own hearts that their attitude toward the racial issue and the demonstrators was the 'right' one. The terrifying thing about this is that the woman was undoubtedly sincere. Every time the Klan has a meeting in our area, the proceedings are opened with an invocation by an ordained minister.

Three of the students had to be taken to the hospital for treatment of ammonia burns before being brought to jail. One of the other girls—a student from Duke University in Durham—was in considerable pain when she arrived in our cell because her long hair was saturated with ammonia and her scalp was burning. We washed her hair as best we could in cold water with no soap, but the fumes stayed with us all night, making our eyes water and our throats burn.

In another part of the basement, out of sight but within our hearing, was the men's cell. At midnight, the men and boys serenaded us with *Auld Lang Syne*, and we spent the rest of the night singing freedom songs and hymns back and forth to each other. We had fifteen women in our four-inmate cell, and the men were even more crowded. No one slept much, but at least we were warm.

Being in jail, for the benefit of those who have never had the experience, is no fun. I have often heard cynics in our area claiming that the students liked going to jail and only did it to 'act smart.' I find this impossible to believe. Aside from the physical discomforts and deprivations of jail (and I have been told that the Chapel Hill jail is one of the 'nicest' in the state) the psychological effect of being incarcerated is terribly painful. One is totally cut off from the world and as the hours and then the days pass, everything on the outside fades within one's consciousness to the point of unreality. It is hard to believe that there are still streets filled with sunlight and people beyond the confining walls, and even my own children became vague beings from another life to me in the five days I was locked up.

On January 2, 1964, we were taken upstairs to Recorder's Court for hearing. Let me explain here that our 'crimes'—trespassing and resisting arrest—are listed on the books as misdemeanors and until the summer before had been punishable by a fine of up to $50 or a sentence of up to thirty days in the county jail, or both. During the summer of 1963, when the civil rights demonstrations hit an all-time high in the state, the laws were changed so that the penalties imposed were increased to up to two years imprisonment and a fine in any amount in the discretion of the court on each count; a stiff penalty for an act which is legally in the same category as dropping litter on a public highway. Our lawyer, C. C. Malone, Jr., requested jury trials for each of us and were were released on $150 bonds until the spring session of Orange County Superior Court should convene in Hillsboro, North Carolina.

I discovered when I returned to my home and my daily life that when an older, established white person involves himself in the civil rights struggle, he bears a greater onus than the young white student does. The public here believes that the white students in the movement (the majority of whom are actually Southerners) are 'beatnik' types from far-away-north places who do what they do out of irresponsibility and a desire to attract attention, rather than form any deep-rooted personal conviction. But when a 'matron' from an expensive house in a good part of town becomes involved, her motives are not quite so easy to write off, and the public is therefore more affronted. Many of my townsmen found it especially hard to forgive me for going to jail because I am the mother of four children. I found it especially hard to forgive them for permitting me to on the same grounds. My children, I am proud to say, were proud of me.

By this I do not mean to imply that I have become a pariah. On the contrary, I have many Southern friends who understand why I did what I did and approve of my action. The South, perhaps unfortunately, is not so simple a proposition as it seems from a distance; there are all kinds of people here, just as there are in other places, and Southern society is no less complicated than any other. Luckily for the Southern future, there are many sensitive and intelligent white Southerners whose moral stand on the race issue is completely upright and humane. But there are, of course, representatives of other elements as well. Obscene phone calls have become a commonplace in our lives, and we are often subjected to minor harassments by people who think it scandalous that a *mother* would risk her position in the community and therefore her children's social comfort by taking a public stand. My sincere belief is that in fact my children would have been made a great deal more unhappy if their parents had turned out to be incapable of backing up their beliefs with acts.

In April, all of the civil rights defendants who had been arrested in Chapel Hill appeared in Superior Court before Judge Raymond Mallard. Judge Mallard has had extensive experience in trying civil rights cases,

and I am sure that this is why the powers that be selected him to hear ours. Judge Mallard is extremely well-versed in the law and is considered to be one of the keenest men we have. On the bench, he is a stern man, with an almost autocratic manner, and when he is scheduled to hear a case everyone, from the clerks and bailiffs up to and including the prosecutor, trembles a bit in his boots. In my own private opinion, he is a man with one irrational flaw in his intellectual process, and this flaw involves the preservation of the status-quo here in the South. Whereas he handles other criminal cases competently and sometimes even brilliantly, his attitude in any case involving the civil rights movement is far from my idea of a proper one for an 'impartial' judge to assume, and I have often seen him visibly angry and emotionally involved when dealing with defendants who seek to change the way of life he was reared to endorse.

Raymond Mallard is a middle-aged man with iron gray hair parted just off center and falling in waves at the sides of his head. He wears a London Fog raincoat and drives a sportscar to and from the courts and his home in Tabor City. His personal 'style' would lead one to believe that he is a liberal sort of man, whatever that has come to mean, but one would be very wrong in that assumption. One night, during the period that the special civil rights session of his court was convened, Judge Mallard was invited to speak to a group of Future Farmers of America. The following day, the newspapers reported that he had told these youngsters that he had heard that all of the civil rights demonstrators were paid six dollars a day for their efforts on the picket lines. It was quite a joke among some of the more indigent student defendants that somebody or other must have mislaid the pay envelopes because they had never received this remuneration, but I must confess that I found it not at all funny. I was under the impression that a judge never discussed any aspects of cases in the process of being tried, and I knew for a certainty that no one I knew—and I knew dozens of the people involved—had received any money whatsoever for their participation in the movement. At the time, I thought it entirely reprehensible for him to say any such thing to a group of youngsters, and I still do.

During the course of that first session, Judge Mallard repeatedly remarked that he found it 'passing strange' that so many of the student defendants were from outside the immediate area. This, coupled with his meticulous questioning of convicted defendants with reference to their parents, religious background, et cetera, left me with the impression that he felt that all these young people were part of a sinister plot or conspiracy to send professional agitators disguised as students into our area to stir up unrest and strife. Actually, very few students have the opportunity to attend college in their own home towns, and I found it passing strange that Judge Mallard didn't seem to know this.

District Solicitor Cooper, who was to prosecute our cases, put all of our names on the docket, which meant that all of us who were free on bond had to appear in court on the chance that our case would be called. If one of us had been called and was not there to answer, his bond would have been forfeited and he would have had to await trial in jail. Because of this peculiar circumstance, there were four or five hundred defendants in the courtroom. Judge Mallard announced his own rules concerning courtroom behavior on the first day, and on the second or third a crudely lettered notice of these same rules was posted on the courtroom door. Among other things, Judge Mallard forbade reading, writing, chewing, talking, 'moving around,' eating, drinking and laughing in his courtroom. He then stationed several embarrassed-looking deputy sheriffs in the aisles to act as proctors. Any infractions of these rules would allow Judge Mallard to cite the offender for contempt of court, which could lead to a fine or immediate incarceration in the jail across the street. Needless to say, we all tried to be very quiet and immobile during the long, crowded hours in court, but even so, a few of our number were hauled forward for various reasons. One of them was sitting next to me, and his offense was reading a textbook.

The session began with those people who had participated in street demonstrations and had been charged with obstructing traffic. This particular charge is not defensible in the way that trespass is, and the actions of those charged with it were, in my opinion, ill-advised. But I respect their right to choose their own form of protest and take whatever reasonable consequences they must for it. In any case, after much behind-the-scenes discussion and in light of the fact that there were over a thousand cases to be heard, the defendants waived their rights to jury trials and entered the plea of *nolo contendere,* hoping for light fines and sentences of perhaps thirty days for their misdemeanors. Several of the students involved told me that they thought this would be their punishment if they would cooperate to the extent of eliminating the time and expense to the state involved in jury trials. They pleaded no contest, which leaves the disposition of the case up to the judge. We all sat in stunned silence when Judge Mallard began sentencing these young people to terms up to two years and fines of hundreds of dollars. The tragic thing about this maneuver is that, once sentenced, a defendant who had pleaded no contest has no grounds for appeal.

Also in the early session, a few white professors from Duke University and the University of North Carolina at Chapel Hill who had demonstrated with the students were tried, by jury, on trespass counts. The first of these was the trial of William Wynn, an associate professor of psychology at UNC. During his trial, Judge Mallard appeared to interpret every action of every person in the courtroom as being an act of insolence and a showing of contempt for the processes

of the court, and the atmosphere was very tense. At the close of the trial, when the jury retired late in the morning to deliberate, Judge Mallard remained on the bench, which technically meant that all of the rules of the court were still in force. However, everyone excepting the defendant and court officials were free to leave the courtroom, and most of us did. Professor Wynn remained seated at the defense table for several hours while nothing was being done or said, and finally Mr. Malone requested the court that Professor Wynn be allowed to move from the table. Judge Mallard granted this request, provided that Professor Wynn did not leave the building.

Professor Wynn stretched his legs a bit in the silent courtroom and then sat down quietly on the front bench where someone had left a newspaper, and absentmindedly raised it to his eyes to read. He was immediately brought by the deputy before Judge Mallard (still sitting on the bench in the nearly-empty courtroom), who severely reprimanded him for flagrantly and contemptuously breaking an order of the Judge in the presence of the Judge, by reading. The following day he was served with a contempt citation and later found to be in direct and 'contumacious' contempt of court and fined ten dollars.

The case had been given to the jury in the morning, and just before the noon recess Judge Mallard had them brought back in and inquired of the foreman their numerical standing. The jury—which was composed of ten white men and two Negroes—stood at ten-to-two for conviction. Judge Mallard excused them for lunch and when they returned at 2:30 p. m. they resumed deliberations and remained until a few minutes before six p. m. At this time, Judge Mallard again inquired how they stood and the foreman again replied that they were stuck at ten-to-two. They were excused until seven for dinner and then resumed deliberations until about ten-thirty p. m. The foreman reported no change in their standings, and it was obvious to all of us in the courtroom that there wasn't going to be any change even if Judge Mallard kept them locked up for a week. Normally, particularly in the case of a mere misdemeanor, the court will inquire after a reasonable length of time if there is a possibility the stalemate can be broken, and if the reply is negative, a mistrial will be declared. But this jury was ordered to resume deliberations the following morning at nine-thirty, and in all was allowed to remain in actual deliberation upon a misdemeanor charge for a total of over nineteen hours before Judge Mallard exercised his 'discretion' to declare a mistrial.

Ultimately, Professor Wynn was retried and he and all of the professors were found guilty and given active sentences, unless—and here Judge Mallard would adopt a tone which reminded me of a kindly uncle—they would agree to promise to never again intentionally break the laws of the state for any reason. This, of course, would include never again participating in any demonstration which could lead to their arrest on trespass charges. One of the men accepted the terms, thinking of his wife and child, who could not survive financially for two years without a breadwinner. The others appealed to the State Supreme Court and were allowed free on bond until they could be heard there.

They did not get to my case during the spring term, nor did they call me during the summer term. When the Civil Rights Act was passed, I thought the charges against me would be dropped. The District Solicitor of neighboring Guilford County announced that he was dropping similar charges against defendants from Greensboro demonstrations, but our Solicitor Cooper allowed as how he didn't see any reason to drop the charges against us. Thusly, still technically prisoners of the state of North Carolina, we entered the fall of 1964.

Until my experiences as a civil rights defendant, I had never seen a court in action excepting in the movies or on Perry Mason. I had always thought that the function of the judge was to interpret the law and act as a *neutral* party representing the interests of that law, while the two lawyers represented the two sides of the case at issue. My conception of the judge's role—in our state at least—has changed considerably after watching Judge Mallard in operation all those many long days. As another example of what I witnessed, let me cite the case of young Gary Blanchard.

Mr. Blanchard was a witness in the Wynn trial, and was not himself directly involved in any of the demonstrations. During the course of his questioning, it came out that he was co-editor of the *Daily Tarheel*, the UNC campus newspaper, and that he had written an editorial about what he called the 'nonsense' of Judge Mallard's courtroom restrictions, which I have outlined for you above. Solicitor Cooper then asked if Mr. Blanchard thought that the court, as represented by Judge Mallard, was in fact 'nonsensical.' After much confusion, knowing that he was damned if he did and damned if he didn't, Mr. Blanchard conceded that yes, he did think some of the rules were 'nonsensical.' Later on, a citation for contempt of court was issued and served upon this witness, and Mr. Blanchard was instructed to appear before Judge Mallard to answer this charge of contempt for having stated such an opinion in the presence of Judge Mallard!

The student editor turned up early in the morning, with counsel, and Judge Mallard (who appeared to have had some second thought during the night) graciously decided not to punish him after all because Mr. Blanchard was obviously 'immature' and several other pitiable things. Thus Gary Blanchard was publicly humiliated for exerting the traditional American right of freedom of the press, and was, at the same time, left without any method whatsoever of defending himself in the eyes of the public. The Affaire Blanchard is just one of many examples I could choose to illustrate what appeared to me to be a musical-comedy atmosphere in Judge Mallard's courtroom. As entertainment, it was fascinating; as a court of law it was simultaneously absurd and terrifying—and I am not unaware of the fact that by writing this I am putting myself in exactly the same position as poor Mr. Blanchard.

Not long ago, some people I know had a party in a house out on a rural road in Orange County. Most of the guests were students and faculty, and some of the students came from the local Negro college. Late in the evening, two carloads of intoxicated white men drove past the house and dishcarged at least one shotgun into it. Later on, they came by foot and surrounded the house, shouting obscene remarks at the guests. One of the hosts called the police—in this case the Orange County Sheriff's Office—and by the time the officers got there, the situation had developed into a kind of free-for-all, with the intruders actually in the house and gunshots flying. The deputies broke it up, sending the guests home and arresting two or three of the intruders for 'forcible trespass'—a more serious charge than simple trespass. This past October, a trial was held in the case and the ring-leader of the group was found guilty and fined $25.

North Carolina is properly considered to be one of the most moderate and forward-looking Southern states, and in terms of the legal aspects of the racial issue, it is as different from Mississippi as it is from New York. The physical brutality practiced by some police departments in the South is well-known to any headline-reader, and I am glad, at least, to be able to say that I have never witnessed any of that in our area. But the more subtle intimidations practiced by our court system and law enforcement officers can also be frightening. During the fracas outlined above, one of the deputies told the complaining host that he wouldn't have troubles like that if he just wouldn't invite any 'niggers' to his parties. All of this, you understand, involves a private citizen's right to entertain privately on private property, and has nothing whatsoever to do with public accommodations or anything specifically outlined in the Civil Rights Act. It's an odd feeling to know that such basic rights as these may not be protected by the men my taxes help to employ.

Another example of what I think of as our 'quiet intimidation' involves a young woman here in Durham and our old friend Judge Mallard. The young woman wrote a letter to Judge Mallard, wondering how she, as a Southern wife and mother of three children, could instill respect for the law and the courts in her children when such activities as his existed in the courts of what is supposed to be the most enlightened state in the South. Two days later, she was terrified by a visit from two agents of the State Bureau of Investigation, who wanted to know why she was threatening a Superior Court judge.

Certainly it is true that society must have courts to

protect itself from law-breakers—but it is equally true that sometimes the law-breakers desperately need and deserve society's protection from the courts. That such an injustice as the sentencing of a young civil rights demonstrator to twelve months at labor for the misdemeanor of obstructing traffic can exist alongside the nominal fining of a gun-wielding intruder is something which should concern every citizen of every state in our nation. If our laws and representatives of the law cannot give equal protection to every citizen, then America is never going to solve her domestic problems, no matter how much political or social action the struggle may generate. Now that we have passed a Civil Rights Act, it is up to us—the private citizens—to set about putting our own houses in order. The states that clamor most about their sovereign rights are those states which do the least to protect their citizens equally. I submit that the citizens of those states who do not wish to see the federal government 'usurping' their prerogatives rally themselves around the cause of doing their jobs and meeting their responsibilities in such a way that no one will have to do it for them.

And I further suggest that citizens of the other states —north, east and west—familiarize themselves with their own state laws and legal systems to find out if their basic rights as taxpayers and citizens are, in fact, being properly protected. There must be millions of citizens who are—as I was—abysmally ignorant and unbelievably naïve about their own legally-guaranteed rights.

Almost two years have passed since that New Year's Eve I spent in jail. In 1964 the Supreme Court announced that it was their opinion that all civil rights defendants who had engaged in peaceful demonstrations and still had trespass charges pending against them should be released from bond and the charges dropped. The students whom I knew who actually went to prison have all been released by now by one means or another, and—excepting any repercussions from this article—I seem to have escaped the clutches of Judge Mallard and Solicitor Cooper. Looking back, I do not of course regret any of my actions, but I must admit that I don't like jail 'one bit' as my youngest boy says, and am very happy not to have to go back. But the passing of the Civil Rights Act, which was a tremendous victory for the cause of justice, is just a beginning. There is still much to do, and most of it needs doing within the framework of the courts and the law. The law is merely a set of rules and regulations invented by men, and not a divine edict handed down to us by any Godly hand. As it was invented by men, it can and sometimes should be changed by men. As Henry David Thoreau said, "We should be men first and subjects afterwards. It is not desirable to cultivate a respect for law so great as our respect for the right."

●●●

Honest Praise

She moves through night rooms like a wraith,
benevolent fingers feeling out the dark,
bumping no spiteful corners of odd furniture
and lifting no sleeper's scalp by scraping chairs
across cold floors.

    She is, as sure as God,
taking care of things, though we neither hear
nor see her going. She soothes the child,
cradling his nightmare into trusting sleep;
she hushes the barking dog in quietest ways;
she brings milk bottles through the door of morning
without a tinkle.

    So when she says to me
smiling like sunshine though pregnant as a cloud
How is the breakfast?, though the toast is burned
and the oatmeal is too dry, I know she means
Praise me; and I do. And I am true.

Edsel Ford

"CHARGE."

-A. HILL."

Canned Goods

My belly full of this domestic life
I stalk the kitchen, hungry for sharp knives.
Or poison. My cat, content with all nine lives,
Gets in his licks. I want to leave my wife,

To hit the alleys with him where he howls
The stupid moon, claws over garbage cans,
Toms every Tabby. The shrivel's in my glands:
I'm fixed. He goes alone. I move my bowels.

He'll come back in the morning, for his milk,
Evaporated, chock full of goodness,
On the same shelf whose plenitude I bless
And lift a can from now. I'm of his ilk.

Sweet Life, the label says. I wonder whose.
Inside the tin, where it's all over, peas
Dumbhuddle in their well-arranged repose.
Out here, I'm in the dark. I have to choose.

Fall Practice

Some after a night of sex, some hungover,
Some tanned, some fat, all still half asleep,
They'd sit around and give each other lip
Before padding up and cleating the summer clover
The field had grown to cover last season's dust.

"Her? Aw, man, that chick's a highway, I oughtta know,
I've driven it." "You gotta taste
That stuff, grow whiskers on your ass." "The best
I ever had was. . ." and so forth. The old show.
A bunch of scrubs bucking for first team berth.

I couldn't believe their talk. They'd cat all night
Yet next day hit the dummies, digging the turf,
Sweating, driving themselves for all they were worth
Into each other like bulls, brute against brute.
Whatever they got, girls, drunk, it wasn't enough.

It went on like that, late August through November.
Though I was the quarterback, the thinker
Who directed that beef, split ends, and set the flanker,
I worked at the center's butt, and I remember
Being primed for the big game, hungering for the cup.

Kissing Kin

Grandfather, your cigars
Secreted a soggy affection
Which you passed around, lip to lip,
With the largesse of body odor
When relatives came to visit.
You'd greet us at the door
Your mouth already pursed
From the glowing fifty-cent stump,
As if honoring a family custom
And sucking your private pleasure
Were all one.
Though no one would admit it
Or bother to understand
We were offended,
And knowing what to expect
The best we could hope for was
You'd have your teeth in.

I remember this
Unpleasant ritual
Because you left little else
To remember. I sometimes felt,
Entering your house,
That I had been passed around
At someone's birth, or that to you
We all were stuffed cylinders
Whose arms and legs would slough off
When we were bought or sold,
As my father was sold out
In your will because you thought
He would go out, like a cigar,
Without your scratch to light himself.
Which is to say you thought
Of him as you thought of yourself.
It came to that, old leaf,
And it is no small thing
That as you were kissing us
You rolled your own
Life into cold ashes and smoke.

Grindl

for Binford, at nine

I know it's safe. That's Imogene
Coca, and they're in a studio,
And that's really her face
And she looks monstrous because
It's her business.
Don't be scared. I was only kidding
When I told you that Beowulf story.
It's just a story,
Believe me.

I couldn't tell you the truth:
That Beowulf and his friends
Were having more than one mead
And watching Grendel on TV
The night Grendel left home
To sneak up on his enemies
On his enemies' day off.

        So Grendel,
Disguised as himself, swam up
To the top of the sea and landed
Not at all tired. Dripping weeds
He stalked off through the forest
To his enemies' big house. The camera work
Was terrific, and all the boys
Around the set thought the suspense
Was killing when Grendel knocked
At the door, which was unusually polite
For him to do. Then they were speechless
As Grendel bashed in the door
And swallowed each of his enemies
Whole.

In those days there were no commercials.

Fireworks

I was told the sky was bright as day,
Or a million days pressed so tightly
Into one July night that they exploded
And rained, like a blessing from old heaven,
And all the eyes who saw it,
Including your mother's, came away
Full of visions, and the luster of darkness
Blown inside out shone on them
So brilliantly that the display
Seemed to last and last on into
The next day.

Sitting beside your bed, I watched those
Fabulous lights flicker all over the walls
And ceiling, and had trouble telling
Them from the shadows they brought in.
You rode the double bed like a princess
In a dream, all but lost
In the hollow between the pillows.
You slept without a twitch,
But I couldn't hear your breathing for the noise.

When it was over and your mother
Relieved me I went outside
With echoes in my head and your
Image, daughter, burning in my eyes.
I found above me the same dark bowl
I swim in every night, year in year out,
Leaking a few old stars.

JUDSON CREWS

WHITE

As your flesh
          is
I call it

Flame-like
       noting
at dawn

You doffed
       your night
garments

In the night—
       dolphins
you were after

Not wishing
       to spoil
the gossamer

In all the world
       of salt
and foam and green

IF I SHOULD

Peel out of
       an inhibition
or two

If I should say
       hello
to whom ever

When I feel
       like it
to hell with

Saying hello
       what I mean
to say

Company manners
       are for
company, and you

My dear friends
       are dear
dear friends

SPITTING

In the water
       watching
it flow slowly

Away, seeing
       some sea
creature grab

For whatever
       it is
—What is it?

Here I have
       given
something

Of myself
       I am sure
it is not

Likely
       to change
the tide

Primeval Apollo

Tired of chewing
   On the snake
He thought of something
   He could make

And bending the stick
   He had in his hand
He strung it taut
   With a twisted strand

Then plucked away
   With a gleeful grin
On the only lyre
   That had ever been

Till another savage
   Said, "Come on, boys,
Let's make him stop
   That plucking noise!"

Whereat the gleeman
   Showed his ire
By putting a stick
   To the string of his lyre

Thus making what later
   He would know
As the god-given first
   Almighty bow

And pulling it back
   That bard troglodytic
Enlightened the heart
   Of the first angry critic.

Quite Certain

On the moonlit beach
   Each to each
Their murmuring mixed
   With the scuff of the surf

And songs of The Platters
   Wafted their way
From the gown-swept open
   Deb-haunted dance floor

Where they'd left the others,
   She an athletic
Well-tanned well-read
   Not at all frenetic

Obtuse or loose
   All American Girl,
He happy there
   On the silken sand

And both of them clear,
   Though their eyes were shut,
As to where they were
   And for what.

WALTER H. KERR

This Comic World

1. *The Politician as a Natural Born Astronaut*

Balloons of conversation heat the air,
obscuring but not hiding the cartoon
world which existed before loony moon
talk smogged the atmosphere. Paper worlds tear
with silence pulling at the margins' narrow finger hold. A funny thing will soon
happen on my way to the lunar boon-
doggle. I'll find myself already there,
having taken leave of my ballast at
an age when tongue first curled about a sound.
I stand before you. Marvel at my poise.
As I talk endlessly of this and that,
observe the filibustered air grow round,
lift me through any silent space with noise.

2. *The Herd and the Conforming Scene*

With so much bull, all questioners are cowed,
endorse with silence the stupidest plan,
the assumptions of power, rather than
expose their naked noggins to the crowd,
emerging from humility with proud
forthrightness. The crowd unit is not Man
Cum Laude. Buffaloed into some herd animal,
it never voices thoughts aloud
and what is heard is half believed in spite
of proverbial injunctions our youth
flew like a flag in a rebellious breeze;
now let some goon speak and he becomes right
by default. We follow, if not in truth,
his slightest whim, stampeding on our knees.

Below the Level of the Eye

I crouch behind ramparts of flesh and bone
and gaze through scopes and shutters of the eye,
with wirtap tuned to every pitch in sound
and nostril flared for spoor and rut and death.
The words of brass are bitter in my mouth.
I reach for love and only touch myself.

The only universe I know is self,
high-strung upon the galaxies of bone,
the deeps of flesh; the rest is word of mouth,
the hearsay of my ground glass stalk of eye.
The only evidence I have of death
is evidence that courts might not think sound.

In deeper waters than this world I sound
the depths of being, finding but myself,
a living island in a sea of death.
I work my midnight fingers to the bone
unmasking knowledge, but only find an eye,
red-rimmed with doubt, a nose, an ear, a mouth.

The platitudes and nothings that I mouth
are but a graveyard whistling and a sound
of exile from the island of the eye
from which I call for rescue to myself,
surrounded by my seas of flesh and bone.
I call for rescue and I call for death.

The cells of bone and flesh all mimic death.
My tongue turns into nothing in my mouth.
This is a scarecrow world of skin and bone,
a universe of fury, fret and sound.
I turn to silence, then I find myself
awake below the level of my eye.

My self is not this body, not this eye
that gazes with a half-closed lid at death.
This universe of flesh I call myself
is but a figment of my lying mouth
which calls forth visions from a sea of sound
and crucifies them on a cross of bone.

I break the bars of bone but find no I.
I muffle sound but hear no word of death.
I close my mouth and there I find myself.

Before Sleep

Lifting my arm, I feel the blood
rush to my elbow, swarm
inside my breast. Counting
the uneven rhythm of my heart,
one by one the lights
go dark, go dark and dying.
Transfixed, I hear
the breathing terror
in the room,
the drowning sound
of sleep.

Observing the Plants
at a State College

With glossy care the state preserves
its academic plants. Succinctly pruned,
devoid of green, they blossom well, observe
each law of stalk and thrust to bloom

sequentially all year, persuaded by
fluorescents overhead to put forth more
than seasonal delight. The sky,
a clerical mistake, will never pour

and ravish them, nor will it burn
the shining faces, reddened underside.
Protected by these walls, they learn
to shape their leaves and hide

their roots inside the coarser clay.
Touched by wind, their tentacles erupt to yes,
and motion in affirmative they praise
the thinking air and wait for it to pass.

Medusa

The snakes sleep in the warm wind of my scales,
waiting for Perseus, who comes by choice
not as a lover, cursed by my beauty
or the bright snare of my voice,
but for precedence: my virgin head
and the wintry chime of my breath.

Even here I have heard of his shield:
Metal as broad as the light
that breaks over Olympus. His body
is Greek, proud and ripe
for a woman.

And I, more like stone than a woman,
so cold; no man warms my thighs
or pulls me to bed, catching the naked
design of his love, nor desires
my mouth more than death.

My darlings are waking from sleep,
they pull at the nape of my neck,
their sweet coils and bright mouths
stretch in the dark,
and all the coiled forests of my love
shine in the air as we wait.

ADRIANNE
MARCUS

PAUL NEWMAN

Letter from Puerto Rico

To Gene Cantelupe

The thunder smells of ozone,
through a crack a drip falls steadily,
water forms in pools and runnels
on the tiles and rattles in a bucket.
You know, Gene, how I told you Czechs
who live like Vlasek (whether he killed
that girl or not) are victims of their pride,
destroying their desire, because it will not
let them be themselves? Here on this island
everything is chaste and vital
as that fight your parents must have had
to be themselves while finding out
American means something else—more,
perhaps, or less—but first a sacrifice.

Hibiscus is blooming everywhere, and jasmine
in our alley blooms so sweetly in the night
you can smell it while you're sleeping.
Rain rushing down in the orange leaves
makes a rustle in the afternoons,
right now the thunder sounds like falling stones
hitting the roof among the mangos
knocked down by the shots of ragged boys
who shake them loose before they're ripe,
then leave them in the streets to rot.
It's a game with them, their way of proving
what they are, although they pay with empty bellies.

Like yourself, I'm working at a statement,
trying to make it plain, but couldn't do it
till I tried it like your parents did
in coming to the States (as I came here).
Perhaps this means that nothing else can help us
in the face of what made us, being Americans.

The Birth

The dry pine needles look red in the rain,
the grass is red too with more yellow in it,
there is the smell of rain and not much sound
except a heron complaining on the river.
It is nearly Christmas and the year
coming with a silent joy
certain death. The new year, just as certain,
full of sadness. I walk along the road,
the rain has made little dents in the sand,
the ruts are white. The needles smell a little
of the rain. On the trees they are wet
and they shake drops on you if you brush
against them. I have walked through the fields
and am covered with beggar's lice.
Climbing a pile of trees that had been ripped up
and torn to make a clearing in the woods, I tripped
and I could smell the sassafrass as I fell there
among the scraped trunks and the dry leaves.
I got up and walked on toward the creek.
There are piles of oysters there projecting
out into the marsh. The ground is higher
where the live-oaks and the yaupon crowd
you over toward the edge, and the myrtles
and the bays have filled up all the space
and scattered their dry leaves on the ground.
I picked a bay leaf and smelled it
and crushed it between my fingers.
It was large and smooth and looked
as though it had been varnished
over a dark cheerful green. It was dry
like the sharp-edged holly leaves
that also grow there. I walked along
the crushed oyster shells and white clam shells
looking for bits of Indian pottery
and climbed over an arm of the marsh
on the branches of the felled trees
and walked along among the small palmettos
each holding up a fan on a single stalk
and the yuccas with white hairs growing
from their blades, and I followed the bank
of the high ground covered with yellow leaves,
a live oak grew over a little pool
filled with bubbling and swirling water.
I though it must be marsh gas, but as I leaned
against a tree it stopped and as I looked through
the white air and the leaves and down
at its reflections I could see myself
standing there above the grasses and the trees
reflected in the water. Then I moved
and all the water came awake again
struggling and swirling and I realized it was minnows.
I walked down to the river's edge
crossing the mud and sand with the burrows
of the fiddlers. I could feel a light wind
from the ocean. The air was white
and the sun made little warmth and you could
see that civilization had made some progress here.
Then I walked back, the rain coming down
and shaking off the pine leaves and I thought
my mother would have liked this, or is it
something within her mated to this country
that she did not understand I feel now,
and the red grass has seeds I see now,
dry fluff that grows within the leaves,
the little seeds each fastened to a bit
of cotton, and they go off floating
when you brush them with your fingertips.

A. R. AMMONS

First Carolina Said-Song

as told me by an aunt

In them days
   they won't hardly no way to know if
     somebody way off
     died
       till they'd be
      dead and buried

     and Uncle Jim

hitched up a team of mules to the wagon
and he cracked the whip over them
    and run them their dead-level best
the whole thirty miles to your great grandma's funeral
     down there in
     Green Sea County

     and there come up this
awfulest rainstorm
    you ever saw in your whole life
    and your grandpa
    was setting
    in a goatskin-bottom chair

and them mules a-running
and him sloshing round in that chairful of water
     till he got scalded
     he said
     and ev-
     ery
anch of skin come off his behind:

we got there just in time to see her buried
   in an oak grove up
   back of the field:
it's growed over with soapbushes and huckleberries now.

Second Carolina Said-Song

as told me by a patient, Ward 3-B,
Veterans Hospital, Fayetteville, August 1962

    I was walking down by the old
Santee
   River
    one evening, foredark
    fishing I reckon,

    when I come on this
swarm of
bees
    lit in the fork of a beech limb
    and they werz

    jest a swarming:

    it was too late to go home
    and too far
and brang a bee-gum

    so I waited around
    till the sun went
down,
most dark,

    and cut me off a pinebough,
    dipped it in the river
    and sprankled water
on'em: settled'em right down,
    good and solid,
about
    a bushel of
   them:

    when it got dark I first cut off
the fork branches and
then cut about four foot back toward
    the trunk
and I
    threwed the limb over my shoulder
    and carried'em home.

Dividing Line on a Note Inside

the persecuted movement
the results of hate
   the new doctrine
   the search for junk
the best stuff
the wet ways
  the vase with nothing in it
  the wives who cant
there was a girl
i used to go with
   she could in 5 minutes
   i married her
& she could not
anymore
politics?

   stability & struggle
   momentary lust —five min. marxism
   (theory)

the only judgment trusted here
something I cannot press
   maybe flight of dark wings
   in lungs
dying

& weapons to goforthwith brutally lost
defensive agents
always talk
   sentiment & THEIR logic
but

come on buddy tell me What happens
when I want to know some
thing ?

CLARENCE MAJOR

●●

Tear on Dotted Line

   I need to do this
   because of the sad sadness
they made it too green
for me this year next year
   the thing to do mother
   is never give up your belief
    in those lies
    you grow stronger
  with them bitches
  and I just can't forget
  how there is nothing
    behind that sheet
    on the porch flapping
    nothing at all not even wind
it's just now we need
(not this table) no chair
that camera takes good pictures
    but nobody ever saw a
    little boy bent double
    looking back thru his legs
  with upsidedown face
  grinning toothless—that's me mother O hostility
  you iceberg you, that's
    exactly what I told her
    while she kept saying Open Here
    Open Here
    Open Here
until I finally caught on

JACK KEROUAC

●●●

A Curse at the Devil

Lucifer Sansfoi
　　Varlet Sansfoi

Omer Perdieu
　I. B. Perdie
　　Billy Perdy

I'll unwind your
　guts from Durham
　　to Dover
　　and bury em
　　in Clover—

Your psalms I'll 'ave
　engraved
　in your toothbone—

Your victories
nilled—
You jailed under
a woman's skirt
　　of stone—

Stone blind woman
with no guts
and only a scale—

Your thoughts & letters
Shandy'd about
　　in *Beth*
　　　(Gaelic for *grave*).

Your philosophies
run up your nose
again—

Your confidences
and essays bandied
　in ballrooms
from switchblade
　to switchblade

—Your final
duel with
　sledge hammers—
Your essential
secret twinned

to buttercups
& dying

Your guide to 32
European cities
scabbed in Isaiah
—Your red beard
snobbed in
　Dolmen ruins
　in the editions
　of the Bleak—

Your saints and
Consolations bereft
—Your handy volume
rolled into
　　an urn—

And your father
　and mother besmeared
　at thought of you
　th'unspent begotless
　　crop of worms
—You lay
　there, you
　queen for a
　day, wait
for the "fen—
　sucked fogs"
　to carp at you

Your sweety beauty
discovered by No Name
in its hidingplace

　　til burrs
part from you
from lack
of issue,
　sinew, all
　the rest—
Gibbering quiver
　graveyard HOO!

　The hospital
that buries you
　be Baal,
　the digger
　Yorick
& the shoveler
　groom—

My rosy tomatoes
pop squirting
　from your awful
　rotten grave—

Your profile,
　erstwhile
　　Garboesque,
　mistook by earth—
　eels for some
　　fjord to
　　　Sheol—

And your timid
　voice box
　strangled
　by lie-hating
　earth
　　forever.

May the plighted
　Noah-clouds
　　dissolve in grief
　　of you—

May Red clay
　be your center,
& woven into necks
　of hogs, boars,
　booters & pilferers
　& burned down
　with Stalin, Hitler
　　& the rest—

May you bite
your lip that
　you cannot
　meet with God—
　　or
Beat me to a pub
　　—Amen

The Almoner,
　his cup hath
　　no bottom,
　nor I
　　a brim.

Devil, get thee
back
　to russet caves.

to ginsberg and ferlinghetti
a myriad of howling
        judges of morality
        improving conduct
        from their benches
        hiding wenches
under flowing robes of solid black
and judgments of the same color.
so to g. and f. and father walt
and d. h. and h. m. and j. k.
        and jesus,
who died to save us from that kinda crap.

THE EARTH WEIGHS

as much as forty-six billion
average-sized refrigerators.
said the appliance salesman.

THE EARTH CONSISTS

of nine hundred seventy million
dumptruck loads of dirt
said the building contractor.

OH WHERE

to set the iceboxes
when they cart the earth away?

i'm tired of conventionality
        and eight-hour days
        and middle-class income
        and the inevitable outcome,
        and two-car families
            in suburban developments
            that never develop

i'm tired of sunday sundays
        one day a week religion
        and easter clothes
        and christmas presents
        and thanksgiving turkey
        and fourth of july firecrackers
            that blow up everything

i'm tired of patriotic unpatriots
        who wave a flag they never see
        and hate for the hell of it
        and fear god
            on sundays
and kill each other
            on tuesdays

i'm tired of everything
        and i haven't seen half of it yet.

Chel leaned against the wall. The mid-sun, shining between the slatted white blinds, striped her cheek. She closed her eyes.

"Are you comfortable?" asked the doctor.

"Yes," her answer, like the slow lisp of a child, came once, and then again, "yes."

The counting began. One, two, five, seven. At the count of seven, she fell asleep. And opening her eyes that were sealed against waking, looked upon the doctor. He had removed his white jacket and sat in his shirt sleeves, holding in his palm a round flat watch, like those grandfathers used to carry. Chel could not blink. She frowned, a little shyly, and followed the dance of the dust motes weaving through slanted beams of light.

"How do you feel?"

"Just fine."

"Are you still comfortable?"

"Yes, very comfortable." She melted into the blank wall and was soon evaporated into sunbeam. Her cells dipped and bloomed in translucent corollas, her blood lisped its dark way through channels and was ejaculated in bright streams over a precipice.

"Hold out your arm. Your right arm."

Obediently and without question, the arm, the right arm, lifted and stiffened. The doctor sat and followed the needle of his watch. Piteously it tore away shreds of time, of Chel's time, and then devoured them politely, obediently. He turned to the girl before him, on the other side of his desk. She sat so quietly, placidly

Chel

HEATHER ROSS MILLER

holding out her arm, like a statue of warm rose flesh left in a ruined garden. He tapped the wrist. He pressed upon firm bone and resilient muscle around which was clasped a thin gold chain of charms. It held. He grasped her arm and tugged, gently at first, then harder. She resisted.

"Why are you holding your arm out like that?"

"Because."

"Because I told you?"

"No, because it feels good."

The doctor snapped shut the watch and began pulling on his jacket. "One, two, three."

Chel opened her eyes again. They felt weak. They felt they might possibly look red and old if she were to examine them in a mirror.

GILBERT CARPENTER

The doctor was standing at the open door, smiling officially.

"See you next Wednesday. And try to remember all we've said."

She went out, heavily, smoothing the wrinkles in her blue smock, and the sun met her in a dazzling flood along the corridor.

2.

At home, on the gallery, the rocker squeaked comfortably and before her the mountains rose in emerald billows, bristling with unruly pine. Bees droned monotonously in the big hydrangeas. She was marooned in a sea of honey. The sun on her face was thick and sweet and smelled of August in the country. It stretched like a lazy beast, a beast furred in gold, claws sheathed, its tawny throat vulnerable. She would be alone this way until six.

"Are you comfortable?" she asked herself. And answering, "Yes, I am comfortable," sank into the heavy sea of honey. All afternoon, she rose and sank, a blue sail blown full by the scent of hydrangea, soaking in the pull of the bees and illuminated under the pleasant indifferent torpor. Inside her, the child trembled.

Slowly, towards the wane of the afternoon, Chel opened her eyes, one at a time, cautiously, peep-eyeing. Over the dark green mountains, the sun spread a thin yellow veil, winking in dust. She was filled with languor and her eyes felt red again. The tissues of her brain echoed with the curlicues of the dense hydrangea and her blood lay flat as the long shadows across the sagging porch.

"Where have you been?"

"Hold out your arm."

"Are you comfortable?"

At six, Roy came, big, exhausted, his shoulders wet. "How's my girl?"

Laboriously, she prepared the supper and set it steaming in bowls on the table. The chianti was bitter. "I don't like it."

"It's just to sip," he said, pouring out a lipful for her glass. "Just to sip."

"But I want to *drink* it!" Chel shook back her hair, long and fine as cornsilks, the stale gold color of vermouth.

"Wine is to sip," Roy insisted. "Beer is to drink. And," he took a bite and chewed thoughtfully and swallowed and continued cheerfully, "we have no beer."

In the night, as Roy slept good-naturedly, one sun-browned arm struck carelessly across her pillow, Chel arose and went out to the gallery where stars blossomed profusely in the black. The rocker squeaked under her and she looked down at her arms folded limply across her thick belly. They were pale. They seemed weak upon the mighty weight of her belly. It was drawing full due. Roy's son would burst forth and blossom like one of the infinitesimal stars in the dark firmament.

"Are you comfortable?"

The honey fell in slow drops, coiling and recoiling, swirling, spinning on an oaken wheel, bubbling in tiny star-specks. Over a hundred miles away, a thundercloud hammered the sky and Chel's white arms felt the vibration.

3.

On Wednesday, she sat before the doctor's desk. He counted. She slept.

"Look at the rosebud in my lapel."

Chel obediently looked.

"It's pink now, but watch it turn into red."

She watched. The small tight bud unfurled and a scarlet glow ignited the points of her eyes and ballooned and usurped the place where the doctor had been.

"Can you hear?"

"Yes."

"What time is it in London?"

She heard the bells ringing sharp and dissonant, sprinkling the hours like flecks of steel grain through the cloudy air. The time was three, then nine, then twelve, not noon and not midnight twelve, but an indiscernible twelve. Chel gave way to the visitation: houses of Parliament, spires of Buckingham where soldiers march in red, a curling strand of Thames.

"Are you comfortable?"

"Yes." Lisping, lisping, these are the first words you ever learned. You saw a red rose and its thorn pricked your fingers and you bled red drops all over your white organdy. Yes.

When Chel waked, he said to her, flushing with pride, "You are a perfect somnambule. You have absolutely nothing to fear. The baby will be born alert and the memory of labor will fade rapidly."

August did not fade rapidly. It burned away unyieldingly, and September came, still burning. The mountains before the long gallery withered. The earth parched hard and pine needles broke with a crisp snap underfoot. All around her, the heavy honey surged incessantly in hues of amber and rose gold, streaked through with sienna, umber, ochre, coagulating to burnt blood, dried drops on a loom of organdy.

"Are you asleep?"

"Yes."

"Where are you?"

"I'm not anywhere yet."

More honey, more heat, accented with the crisp rattle of brown hydrangea and the drone of wearied bees.

"Where are you now?"

"I'm in the cellar. Hiding. They call me 'Rochelle.

Rochelle.' Louder. 'Row-chelle!' How I hate the sound of their voices calling me 'Row-chelle.' "

"Do they find you?"

"No. I slip out and surprise them at their play. I am dirty from the black cellar. My finger nails are ringed in dirt."

"Are you comfortable?"

"Yes."

"Why are you holding your arm out like that?"

A trellis of roses unfurl to the clashing of iron bells. There is a flounce of spotted organdy. *I took a ride on a ferris wheel and I was sick and I tried to jump out and they jeered at me. The pocket on my dress was torn and a fistful of hot cinnamons spilled out.*

"You have a fine healthy boy."

"No. It's impossible."

"Why do you say that?"

"It's not time. I'm still comfortable."

"You have a fine healthy boy."

"I have no child."

4.

Roy entered her room. It was all brightness without sunshine and no dust motes teeming in the air. He held a bouquet of fresh flowers.

"How's my girl?"

Grinning, his white teeth sharp and firm, his big certain hands plumping the pillow, cigars bulging his lapel, he was no more, no less, than Roy.

"I've told everybody." Roy scraped up a chair. He put the flowers on her tray, right between the water vessel and the thermometer. "But, honey, what's his name?"

Chel searched the air for dust. The sun was sterile here. The pillows smelled of carbolic and soap. Roy squeezed her hand. "Honey, what's the baby's name?"

Chel looked at him. Her cornsilk-fine hair felt dry, and her mouth, bitter and disappointing as chianti, cracked with the reply, "I don't know." And she closed her eyes, feigning sleep.

In her white soapy bed, Chel slept. Above and beneath her, thrusting endlessly, were rooms with beds where people slept, grew well again or sickened and died. At 2:00 a.m., the nurse, masked and whisper-soft, appeared with a child in her arm. She wakened Chel.

"Are you comfortable?"

"No."

"Why not?"

"I have this child at my breast. Can't you see! I can no longer hold out my right arm."

When the child had gone away, filled, Chel tried to sleep again. But no honey swam beside her bed, no warm sun melted the sterile dustless air. The easy chain would not unclasp. She held out her arm, her right arm. It faltered in the dim light and fell to her flattened empty belly, a broken wing.

DER TAG

H. ROTH

Joseph Ginger plucked the bow tie, smiling grimly as the elastic pinged back across his Adam's apple. As he walked to the subway, he avoided a closer look at the morning sky; instead he stared down at his shoes, aware only of the high shine upon the leather—proof of his sinking into the soft sands of age. Why fuss with shoes when no one sees them all day and who the hell cares if he's even wearing socks? He must ask Ryan about this preoccupation with shoes. He smiled, for Ginger guessed Ryan's facile explanation . . . "sexual, Joseph, purely sexual."

Summer was the most malevolent season of travel by subway. In the heat festered tunnels, the least effort was a herculean task; the simple act of breathing, the slightly more complicated movement to finalize a

sneeze or cough made his body tremble. Noise boomed like shrill thunder. This time it was even worse than yesterday and the time before that—women smelled like they were in heat, the men had never bathed in their lives; the train lights were daggers piercing every crevice in his body, the train moved jerkily, cursing them all. Finally, allowing himself to be swept out of the train at his stop, Ginger breathed deeply and began the slow walk up the station steps.

The sun revealed how filthy the city was and how dejected were the people who walked on its streets. As was his custom, Ginger stopped off at the dingy luncheonette on the corner. The smell of foul grease flooded his nostrils.

The owner-cook greeted him with a nod and a cup of black coffee. Ginger drank his coffee, left his dime, and strolled out still not speaking a word aloud to the man. Walking up the street, he permitted himself a short whistle. With a lot of bad luck that could well be him mired in a crumby, six stool, four table luncheonette instead of a *palace* like his place. He had once toyed with the idea of the PALACE and he was frequently sorry he hadn't named it that instead of the PINES. He might just change the name but he shuddered to think what Ryan would say. Until he

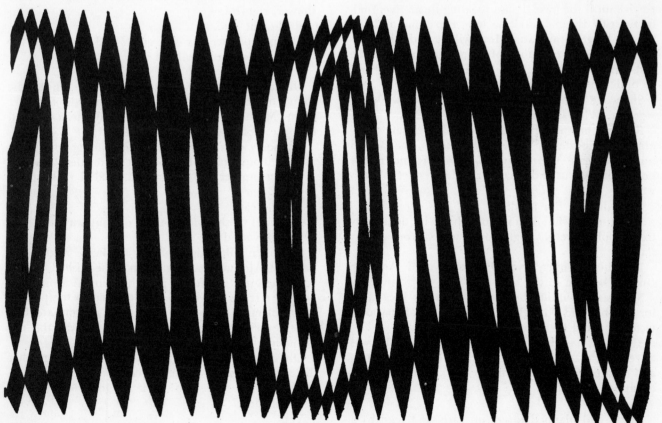

"D-6-65"

MACKEY

got to the bar, Ginger weighed the pleasure of the name to Ryan's taunts; when he opened the door and switched on the lights, he was still smiling, still debating with himself. The grin widened as the air conditioner began to function and he could feel the stifling heat whisking away and his body lightened magically.

Ryan tugged at Marjorie's hair. She moved but relaxed and went back to sleep. Ryan judged by the angle of the sun getting into the window that it was still early—not much after eight, but the day is begun. We must greet it, he whispered into her ear. Greetings, greetings, he shouted toward the window. The girl moved again but was quiet, she was determined to keep her eyes closed. He smiled down at her. Stubborn thing.

Ryan too dozed a while, when he awoke Marco's name was on his lips. I was sleeping too short for a nightmare, why the hell is that pig's name on my mind? He looked at Marjorie, she did not in the slightest resemble Maureen, possibly she could have been their daughter; he brushed away this, other unpleasant thoughts or tried to . . .

But Marjorie did possess one trait of Maureen's: like veteran rodeo performers, they both held on, despite his wildest performance. They would not be thrown silently; they dug their spurs into him, they weakened him for every bucking outburst, and finally he was passive until the next try at unseating them. Eventually, the ride is less brutal, no longer exciting and the fall no longer traumatic. How will it end with us—how will it end, charming Marjorie, he sang. . . . She had turned on her back, her breasts taunted him and he pulled her hair furiously.

She woke with a start, sitting up, pulling her knees together. What's wrong? she yawned.

Russians are planning to kill us, Chinese are planning to suffocate us, the French hate us, the British no longer care what happens, Africa would rather not hear about us and I haven't had my coffee. What's wrong?

She laughed, I'm tired.

He raised his fist, You've no right to be tired, only free people have any right to be weary. You are my slave.

Not this morning, Ryan, I'm really tired. And she sank back down to the bed.

She wasn't kidding but neither was he; he leaned forward but said I'll make coffee today but after you've tasted it you'll be damn sorry.

When he had dressed and looked back in she was asleep. He made the coffee all right but felt grumpy and cheated. The first gulp was black and burnt and he sipped it loudly.

Edgar had planned to get up early and tend to a haircut. The non-union shop opened at 7:30 and didn't get crowded until eight. At 7:30 no one but the owner was there and you could get a good cutting for 75 cents, but once the shop filled, the nervous scab all but tossed you out of his shop. But he slept on, the hell with the haircut—he was becoming increasingly lazy in the morning. The sounds of a fire engine woke him, the nearness of the bells piqued his curiosity and he looked out his dirty window. He saw kids running, some older people shuffling toward the direction of chaos. Up now, he stretched, scratched, stretched again. He opened the icebox and pulled out a container of orange juice.

Over coffee, he told himself his choice of activities: he could call Olivia, he could stop by and waste the day with Estelle (something he had not done for almost six months), he could bother Ryan and Marjorie, he could go to the Pines, he could go get the damn haircut. He decided on the last desperate unspoken alternative—another cup of coffee.

Estelle's eyes were shut tight; the man above her was enjoying himself; she had looked up to find him smiling like a sick Christ, and folded her legs tight about him. Where was she and she lifted herself forward attempting to seize some of his pleasure. Suddenly he was lying across her neck. He whispered, That's all, baby. She touched his back as he slid away, he stopped and pulled at a nipple. He would be still now. Then he broke the silence, I'm going to take a shower, right?

Right, she said.

She put on her dressing gown and went into the kitchen to prepare breakfast.

Olivia slept soundly, she awoke after ten to the sound of a vacuum cleaner functioning in the next room. Mother! she screamed. A small head popped into the room. Mother, you woke me.

I'm sorry dear, but aunt Lil is coming for lunch, and the house has to be ready. It's after ten, Olivia.

As her mother left Olivia said, Shall I pick up my toys, mother?

What, dear?

Nothing, mother; I'll get out of your way.

Thank you, dear.

She often told Edgar of her mother's magnificent deafness. Mother heard only what she wished to and with the great ability to plug her ears at whim had become a tranquil woman not addicted to the pettiest of problems. Olivia had once tried to emulate her, but mother did it so blandly that she was the undisputed champion.

Olivia prepared her own breakfast and when mother discovered this she smiled prettily at her daughter. Olivia returned the smile. I'll be gone for the day.

Edgar, dear?

Yes.

Where are you going?

The museum.

Well, have a good time, dear.

Thank you; my love to aunt Lil.

What would Edgar do if she asked to be taken to a museum? She smoked a cigarette furiously, smirking at herself, for she was nervous. It had been two weeks since Edgar had told her to get out of the apartment, and all she had done during the fourteen days was see movie after movie and devour hamburgers as if they were hail marys.

She worked the lipstick carefully into her lips, she stared deep into the mirror and mouthed herself a warning. Again she checked her lipstick.

Simon laughed at the ringing phone. Drop dead, he screamed at the phone, you dirty coiled bastard, drop dead. He drank his buttermilk loudly; he was very pleased now, for the phone had stopped ringing and the buttermilk was still fresh.

Simon kicked away some of the rubble that was on the floor, tin cans and food, glued dishes sprang from his feet; everything is alive, damn it. He checked his heart, checked his pulse, nodded sadly, blew his nose, scratched at his eyes, forcing tears. I hurt, he cried to himself. He looked desperately for his shoes. He could find only one sneaker. Furiously he threw it at the window and smiled as he heard the shattering noise and then the smack as the glass hit the courtyard.

What the hell, someone screamed.

Drop dead, Simon called down, drop dead.

He ran down the stairs without socks or the damn shoes and bumped into the janitor. The man opened his mouth but Simon spat at him and ran out the door.

I must hurry he told a frightened woman who had dropped a shopping bag at the sight of him. Cursing himself, he paused at the corner. He should have grabbed her bag, she had just come from the market.

This little piggy went to market, went to market, this little piggie went home, this piggie . . . please he told the traffic light, I must hurry. The light blinked at him. WALK, it said, go right ahead. He blew it a kiss.

II

Ginger was furious with them. They only grinned at his lecture.

You guys are a disgrace.

Why, you're not making sense.

Staying up all night, kicking over garbage cans.

Oh c'mon, we didn't. . . .

Well you sure weren't quiet all night, I'm damn sure of that. And your wife.

She's pregnant, Ginger, you can't expect me to lug her around all night.

Ginger shook his head, angry at them, angry too because they were teasing him and it was difficult to

tell how much they were leading him on. But he didn't mind, he liked the three bastards and it would be impossible to make sense of them or to get them angry.

I'll open an ice cream parlor. That'll get you jokers out of here.

Three bottles of warm beer. Quick!

Warm beer it is.

Hey, Ginger, didn't you see Simon?

No, it's not payday today.

You still pay him?

Ginger pointed to the sketches along the wall. Sure, he did a nice job. That picture of the bass jumping out of the water is perfect. I'm going to hang it at home one day.

Take 'em all home.

That's enough of that, you can make fun of his whiskey soured head or his clothes but he loves animals, all them drawings show it. Leave him alone anyway.

We never bothered him; take it easy.

I know. I'm sorry, boys, but I hate even to think of the poor man. What was he doing today?

Racing like hell down Eighth Street.

Ginger shook his head, Maybe he won't be back.

How come Riker's isn't open today?

The manager died.

No kidding.

We damn near died this morning, waiting for it to open.

Hell, Whelans is almost as bad.

I know but it's a block farther.

Christ! The president should get you in the Peace Corps.

Why, man?

He wouldn't go for it but I would. A block farther! You ought to be walking on the Kalahari desert and helping some poor bushman.

Screw the bushman.

Ginger laughed. You would.

Anything, the man swore.

Hey Ginger, you want to hear about the party?

No, he said. But he didn't move away and they began.

Ryan, how long you been here?

Long enough; you were in a huddle over at the other end.

What bums. Are they telling me the truth?

If it's about their work, no, about women, whiskey, true enough.

And everything you say is true, Ginger said a little belligerently.

Ryan paused and said, Everything I say has a strong element of truth to it, very strong.

Ginger cut off a piece of salami. Try it, it's strong as hell.

Sadie said it would discourage conversation.

Is it good?

Sure it's good, why do you think, . . . Oh, no, conversation never stops; everybody's breath stinks anyway.

Not mine, Ryan said, I have only one cavity in my mouth.

What the hell has that got to do with lousy breath?

I don't know but imagine, at my age, one cavity.

When you go to the dentist last?

Hey you really got up cockeyed, want me to go out and come in again?

It's the damn subway ride.

You ought to take the car.

That West Side highway is only for nuts.

Hell, you're a great man for physical fitness. Walk as far as you can then grab a taxi.

I been thinking of that one, that subway is really getting on my back.

It's settled then, Ryan said, what have I got for lunch?

You haven't been here all week.

You mean I can't get lunch?

You can get lunch but what you been doing?

Not anything artistic, fixing up the loft, another week and we'll have a shindig, a private one. You have to be impressed; the place looks like a palace.

Ginger smiled.

Ryan said, Don't you believe me?

Oh sure, what about Virginia ham?

Give me two portions.

O.K.

For the price of one and a half.

Done.

They shook hands solemnly and Ryan called out, Plenty of bread and butter.

Ryan, shut up will you.

Olivia walked along Second Avenue peering into the bakeries and grocery stores. Edgar had gone and she had lost the key. Edgar had anticipated her coming and gone. Where? He had so many places to go and enjoy himself she could only be a fool and walk. She walked quickly now, her tongue slightly out and oblivious of the stares of some young men standing outside a candy store.

The first one stopped her, O.K. pretty lady, spend the day here.

She shook her head, smiling in her fright.

Hey, what nice teeth. Nice, huh Angie?

A fat boy sidled over, a hairy hand touched her hip.

She spit at the hand. The boy raised it.

You bums! a woman screamed down. Walk away lady, I know their faces and their names. You bums! Walk away, Miss, they won't bother you.

She felt a compulsion to bathe right away.

She ran back to Edgar's, hoping he was there.

Marjorie walked into Schrafft's, ordered sliced egg salad with a cup of tea, and waited for the order and for the day's events to come properly into focus. She looked at her hands, squeezed her arm gently; she was indeed alive, indeed unbelievably sitting stiffly in a Schrafft's restaurant about to eat egg salad and a cup of tea. If that was true—and it was, for here was the waitress bringing her order—then all the rest was true. As she ate, she stared at her spoon, saw a part of her face and said to it, and your name is Marjorie, don't forget now Marjorie.

III

Ryan glowered at the empty plate. Ginger took it away, calling back, Coffee?

Sure. A full cup, though, my friend.

Edgar's been in the john a long time.

Yeah he didn't look good, that bitch he's with must be racking him up.

What's wrong with her?

What's wrong? She's a shrew, a virago, she's almost a woman but till she gets there she's going to be hell on wheels.

You mean she'll be out of her moods then?

She may be worth hiding in the john for.

Ryan drank the coffee; it could be hotter.

Edgar stumbled out of the bathroom, his head no better, he felt as if his brain had been felled by the stroke of a woodman's axe. He hated the smug smile on Ryan's face and didn't much care for Ginger's pitying look.

Shut up, both of you.

Ryan pointed to Ginger. Shut up.

Ginger waved a fist, threatening. You shut up, Ryan.

Edgar laughed. O.K., O.K., I'm a fool; just don't look like you know it.

You're not a fool m'boy or you would have never walked into the Pines.

Luck? Edgar disagreed. It was cold I was tired and it was either this place or the drug store on the corner.

And you struck gold.

Nuts.

You didn't meet the girl here, you met her. . .

I know damn well where I met her, friend, at your place, your place.

Ah yes; well keep on your feet, the greatest puncher in the world will eventually tire and collapse in your arms.

Edgar said, Can I have gingerale?

Ryan bit his lip. It's worse than I thought. Gingerale. Is that straight or on the rocks?

Shut up, Ryan; gingerale coming up, Edgar.

Have you been doing any work?

Just on the house, not my own. My show was a success; I told you, didn't I?

What do you mean?

A success, Visorsky finally sold all at his price, the critics are still undecided, which means success.

And you?

56   RED CLAY READER

I have decided to forget the whole thing, the only good thing that came out of it is, no, there are two things, first I'm square with that red and Marjorie is still on my team.

Ginger said, how is she? She was telling me last week she feels lousy. She's been tired a lot, she said if she didn't feel better she was going to see the doctor this week.

I know what the hell it is, you haven't been in here for supper lately.

Of course we haven't. Shit, you're not my yiddisha mamma. I'm a good cook and so is she.

No better than my kitchen.

Hell, you've raised your prices twice this year.

I explained, Ryan, the cost.

I get a better break at home.

Ginger said, Come in every night, I'll give you a ten per cent discount.

Edgar said, You know Olivia is right, you both are crazy.

Olivia is, Ryan began. . .

Yeah.

Forget it. Olivia is your friend and I must like her because you are my friend. That reminds me, did you see that gag in *The New Yorker*? One couple is being introduced to another couple and the introducer is saying, We know you're going to love each other because you're two of our favorite people and they're two of our favorite people.

Not funny.

Christ, Ginger, it's a witty thing.

No it ain't.

You don't get it.

Give it to me.

Christ, it's as if you need a passport to become introduced to somebody you know, you need references to shake hands.

Since when do you read *The New Yorker*? Sam Ryan reading *The New Yorker*.

Today I can't do anything without someone putting me down.

Ginger said, Sir.

Screw you, I'm getting out of here and see a picture of my work, they're reselling the catalogue at the Eighth Street book store.

How much?

A buck.

I'll wait till it's reduced.

Hah, Visorsky won't, made them pay cash for the catalogues, they got to sell it for a buck to break even.

Ginger shook his head.

Ryan pointed to Edgar, Did you know our friend drew the cover for the *Review* this month?

No. Why didn't you say something, Edgar?

I didn't know it was on this month's cover.

You want to walk with me, Edgar?

No thanks; I'm going to a booth and going to sleep.

You're all crazy today.

Ginger spat on the counter in exasperation, everybody was staring at him, Ginger was not a spitter and certainly not a spitter in his place.

I'll tell you something, I ought to lock up between one and four, they do it in Europe, your body is tired, your mind wanders, it's a waste of time.

Maybe.

You say stupid things just to talk, to get through the afternoon.

Ryan said, I never stop talking.

But it makes sense after six.

O.K. I'll shut up till six.

Ginger shook his hand. Thank you, Ryan.

Ryan walked off, not bothering to wave.

Simon stared at the door that confronted him, it would not open at his command and he prepared to break it, but before he slammed into it he remembered that the man inside was his friend. Simon opened the door and fell into the room, he got up slowly.

You O.K., Simon?

Simon is fine.

How about a sandwich?

Simon wants drink.

First some food.

Simon nodded.

Someone was whispering, Simon says do this and that. Hey, Simon. But his friend told them to shut up.

Simon felt safe for the minute, he did not look back but sat on the stool and waited happily for his food.

Eat, the man invited. Nice man.

Simon did not see anybody he knew there, three men far away had yelled at him before but they did not yell now. No one should yell, no one should fight.

How are you fixed?

Simon smiled, wanting to embrace his friend.

Simon thirsty.

A coke?

Simon thirsty.

Only beer then, not whiskey, and just one glass.

Simon felt his body quiver with rage, no one should say no, everything should be yes.

"D-9-65"

MACKEY

Simon thirsty.

O.K., here.

It was cold and his body laughed at him, not this—whiskey.

Shut up, he told his stomach. Drop dead, he told his kidney, piss out the beer and forget it happened.

Here, Simon, the friend said later.

Simon looked at the three five dollar bills, he remembered now what he must do, he tried to pay his friend but his friend would not take the money.

Go home, Simon, rest and eat.

Someone else said, Simon says.

And there was the damn door again, Simon was losing patience with this door that would never open, would not be friendly, it should only be happy, magically the door opened, a man came in and Simon pushed past him.

Hey fellow. . .

Drop dead, Simon called loudly . . . and waved his money at the sky and cursed the sun.

Ginger shook his head, it was good Ryan wasn't there; alternately Ryan was either kind or cruel to Simon, poor bastard, one day they will come with a net and that's all Simon. No one ever knew his story though Ginger had pieced gossip, fact and fiction into a story he liked. Simon had been an artist and a good one, he fell one day—or jumped—from a low story roof and though he wasn't killed the brain didn't function perfectly to say the least, but he sold sketches to the tourists and to bars and made enough to drink on. Ginger looked about. He could have done without Simon, maybe he should lock up; if not lock up go away for a few hours in the day. By the evening nobody cares any more, Ginger nodded, something has to be done about the afternoons.

Olivia pushed the door and looked about desperately, the bartender smiled at her and pointed, He's way in the back, he said.

She smiled thank you and rushed into the back.

Edgar was slumped in his seat cradling an unlit cigarette.

He waved and she sat down.

Oh Edgar, I had the most terrible experience.

He didn't look up. Daddy cut off the allowance.

She found herself crying and amazed he watched her for a few minutes, too startled to offer help or a handkerchief.

I was looking for you all day.

You should have come here.

I was on Second Avenue and some boys surrounded me and. . .

He was sitting up now . . .

One touched me Edgar, I felt like I was surrounded by elephants.

The scum. Let me get you a drink.

No.

A drink will make you forget.

She smiled uneasily, I'm sorry about that night.

Forget it.

And the time before that.

He finally lit the cigarette.

You want to go to my place?

I did before. I want a bath.

O.K., let's go.

No, Edgar, you'd rather stay here.

He looked at her, puzzled. Usually he would but there's something going on here today, this place is as bad as my place.

She said, You're sure?

He took her hand, the nails were long and carefully done. We'll come back later for supper; now let's run out of here.

IV

When Marjorie entered she waved to Ryan but stopped at the bar and began talking very quickly to Ginger. The bartender looked at her. She wasn't drunk but something was wrong. He remembered that look the first few times, months ago when the thing with Ryan was teetering in never-never land. He didn't understand a thing she was saying, she seemed to be letting loose just disjointed phrases. He stopped her talk with a nod.

What's up, chum?

Have supper with us, please sit down and have supper with us.

All right, you order and I'll join you.

Ryan was shaking his own hand.

What did you think of the coffee, love?

Worse than you prophesied.

He laughed happily, Tomorrow you will rise and shine.

She said, I asked Joseph to eat with us.

Good, what are we eating?

Olivia felt something race through her body, all her senses were beginning to sizzle.

Your tub is an antique Edgar, it's practically priceless.

It doesn't leak, Olivia.

Is it clean?

Huh?

I mean has it ever been scoured?

Did you clean it after you finished?

No I. . .

Then it's still filthy.

Olivia was poised, she could let the flames continue or put them out. She saw Edgar beginning to get angry and she withheld her decision.

I'm sorry but I'm hungry, could we eat?

No reason why not.

Ryan held Marjorie's hand. How do you feel?

A little better.

He said, Take your pulse, tell your fortune.

Ginger scowled, A hell of a doctor you'd make.

Bush wah, my bedside manner is impeccable.

Like that shirt, Ginger pointed out.

Well, Marjorie said, can you tell my fortune?

Sure it's. . .

Wrong, she interrupted; it's not my pulse that's my fortune. She raised her voice slightly. It's a baby Ryan, a baby; I'm pregnant.

Ginger started to rise, her eyes implored him to sit down.

Holy Christ.

She said, Anyone giving out cigars?

Ryan took both her hands. That's for after the baby. He pushed some potatoes away from her plate. No more potatoes, Ginger, it's no good for a gal in. . .

Ginger said, You happy Marjorie?

I'm scared.

Ryan said, How about me, am I the father?

She said, Of course.

Merely a rhetorical question, already I am shoved to the sidelines, it was me that caused it, I am the creator and violator. A bottle of California champagne, my good maitre d'.

When he returned Ryan said, Be my best man next week?

Sure.

Ryan leaped on the table and did a commendable jig.

He's disgusting, Olivia pointed.

He's happy, Olivia. How do you show you're happy? Not that way.

I mean do you show it in any way?

Of course I do, Edgar.

I get the feeling you really wanted to see me today, you wanted a lot from me today. Now that you've got it all you're sorry you needed it.

Shall I pirouette after a pleasant day?

Why not? You're going to be a damn boring person before you're twenty-one.

Edgar, why must you defend him?

Why must you attack any action that seems unplanned?

An old man with a young girl, doing the cha-cha on the table.

He's doing the dance on the table of the bar of his best friend for a girl who loves him.

I don't believe it; she can't love him.

Shut up, Olivia.

Edgar, don't throw me out a second time, please. I won't come back next time.

Look girl, he wished to strike and kiss her in the same bewildering response, I didn't toss you out for show, I'm not performing, I don't require deeds committed by whim to make me interesting. I'm sick, but I'm not nasty sick, if you have nothing reasonably nice to say or offer, shut up.

Edgar, I mean it.

Olivia, smile and be beautiful, try a little to understand people, not like them; just give them credit for existing in the same world as you.

She felt a burning spread through her body. She looked at his face almost pleading and said stiffly, Could we go over to their table later?

Yeah, I'd like to, there's something going on tonight and I want to find out what.

Marjorie was washing her face when Olivia came into the ladies' room. Marjorie turned, oblivious of the water that ran down her face onto the wool knit jersey.

It seemed for a crazy moment that the girl was wailing monumental tears but the smile and gay eyes exuded pleasure. Olivia, don't think I'm crazy just for blurting it out, but I am pregnant.

Oh Marjorie, did you want it?

No, I'm still not sure, but Ryan has named it and is busy designing the crib.

Olivia asked, Can I lock the door? I want to talk.

Marjorie nodded.

Marjorie, is something wrong with me?

You don't like Ryan.

I don't like anyone.

It's just you don't give anyone a chance.

You sound like Edgar, Marjorie, I swear. . .

Everyone is nice to you, lovely to you, let some man be a bastard to you you'll see what real selfishness is and you'll see you're not a bitch at all.

Marjorie, you don't understand.

Ryan may even leave me in a few years. But he likes me, Olivia; love is not important. Like is the steady thing that keeps you seeing each other day after day and not throwing up.

Love is nothing?

Love is great, the minutes it exists.

Olivia said, You sound like Ryan and Ginger.

I hope so.

Do you think Edgar has given up?

Edgar won't give up, you'll see.

I'm happy for you.

Marjorie hugged her and both were startled by an urgent knocking at the door.

Estelle was slightly worried, the toreador pants were definitely tight in the seat; she felt the strain, the rush of cocktail parties were adding the pounds. A photographer noticed yesterday, complaining that her face was getting healthy and full. Roy tightened the grip on her shoulder.

Why here, Baby?

Because Baby likes it.

The Penguin is only a block away, or even the Steak Joint. Or Asti's, he tried.

I want to go here, Roy.

He patted her behind. Knowing she hated that, he did it again.

I'll go in alone, she warned.

He pulled his arm away. Go right ahead, Estelle.

Come on, honey, she said, and he opened the door for her. He smiled his I'm-a-winner smile and she felt like scratching his face.

Ginger nodded happily to her.

An old beau? Roy pinched her arm.

I wish he was, he's a human being. Cut it out, Roy.

Roy said, I heard of this place, the Pines, an artist trap.

How many times were you married?

Two. Why?

You're so charming.

You like this place? It's dirty.

It's not; it's a friendly quiet place and the food is very good. So be quiet.

Edgar had a vague premonition that Olivia had crawled out the bathroom window. He looked about trying to find a reason to propel himself from the booth, from Olivia, from the silly cigarette he was holding.

Estelle!

Edgar, sit down dear. Edgar Warren, Roy Benedict. They nodded.

A drinkee for all of us, she giggled.

What do you want?

Edgar measured out the words, A creative drink, a double bourbon with one ice cube.

Are you a writer, Warren?

No, but you're close; it's a William Faulkner drink.

What, Edgar?

After two doubles and two cubes I think I am William Faulkner.

What do you do, sport?

Why, man, I look for my Nobel prize.

The drinks were served and Edgar drank his fast, too fast. This Roy boy is going to make it hell for her later. I'm sorry, he whispered.

Excuse me, Estelle, he lied, but I sold a painting a few weeks ago. I'm still in shock. He rose.

Oh how wonderful, Edgar. I'm so happy for you.

Let me pay, Edgar said.

Roy brushed him aside. Glad to do something for the arts. Drop over anytime, fellow.

Olivia walked right into Ryan's arms.

Is she all right?

What?

. . . a hell of a long time in there, she's pregnant you know.

I know, Olivia smiled; we were just gossiping.

Ryan smiled, I'm like a nervous hen.

Rooster, she corrected.

Right, he said. Olivia, call your friend over and have some champagne. Not French, California—can't spoil it, you know.

Olivia laughed.

She waited patiently while Edgar finished drinking with the man and girl. The girl was obviously a high fashion model and she envied the woman's features. He's slept with her, I know it. Finally Edgar returned with a shy smile.

Old flame?

Yep.

Showing off?

Yep.

I know some good gossip.

Good gossip? Impossible.

Marjorie is going to have a baby.

God, does Ryan? . . . Sure, the dance.

Yes. She's nervous, but he's slap-happy. He asked us to the table for a drink.

You going if he asks us back to the loft?

Yes, is it all right?

Edgar kissed her on the forehead. C'mon, pal.

Edgar was rising to make a toast when a girl in the front screamed, a table turned over. Several people began running and Simon burst into the main dining room waving a pistol. Simon screamed, Cease and desist.

V

Simon saw a stream of things, not people or animals but oddly shaped frighteningly swirly pools of things drawing him deeper and deeper, he must make these things stop. Cease and desist, he called out.

Voices were loud everywhere.

No, he said; shut, shut up.

There was his friend smiling at him.

I came, he said to his friend, to say goodbye and thank you.

To the rest he called out, drop dead. Then he pulled the trigger and felt a wonderful pain swim into him.

Ginger said, I was his friend. I only gave him the money because I felt sorry for him.

Ryan said, I thought he was going to shoot up the place.

Nah, not Simon, he wouldn't hurt anything.

Maybe not, but with a gun, the way he was holding it. . .

He was bleeding so.

Forget it, he won't die, it's damn hard to kill yourself even if you're a nut.

They'll put him away if he gets better.

I'm going to see him.

Ginger, you should have been a social worker.

Ryan, you should have been a bartender.

Edgar said, What should I have been?

A beautiful girl, Ryan said, I like your face.

This is a night for confessions.

Pretzels all around, pass em out friends, tonight I am a great man.

A night for confessions, Edgar laughed. Olivia felt she must join in, show somehow she was alive and there. . .

She asked Ryan, Did you know him years ago, I mean before. . .

Huh? Oh, Simon; he was always nuts, he enjoyed it.

You can't enjoy being that.

Why not, lady? It's your own private zoo, you only answer to yourself.

Olivia bit her lip and ignored Edgar's look. You mean you are not much different.

Ryan smiled crookedly. Not the same, but the same mold. Only he was a lousy painter who turned eccentric to enjoy the shock and attention he got. I'll tell you all something else, he never fell out of any screwy window, he never fractured his skull, he just had so much empathy for living he became a sponge.

I don't believe it.

No damn it, I knew Simon in California. I saw him in Mexico, then when he came to the City, he was just a member of a crummy herd so he became an Albino by painting himself white; he did it so goddamn much the paint stuck.

His place was a pig sty, Edgar volunteered; remember the time we carried him home?

Right, Ryan said, he was a nothing.

That's cruel, Olivia said.

It's pitiful, Marjorie said.

O.K., Ryan patted her hand. O.K., it stinks.

Ginger said, I have to go back to work. He kissed Marjorie, Don't name the kid Sam, that's all I ask.

Ryan laughed It's going to be a girl, a beautiful girl with long black hair and a droopy mustache.

Marjorie smacked his lips lightly. You're terrible, you'll probably be disappointed if she doesn't have a mustache.

She will, Ryan promised, she will, she damn well better.

The bar was noisy but distinct sounds were muffled, mouths were talking, chewing, eating, and Ginger basked in the din. He caressed the top of the cash register that constantly received homage. Ginger sat back, letting the two bartenders do their stuff, and thought of the greasy luncheonette on Eleventh Street; he saw the man in cramped rooms behind the store watching TV until tomorrow. Ginger went to sleep counting off penny candy and was immediately lost in nightmare.

Atop a strong shouldered tree, he watched below him—vultures. They pointed, he feeds upon us for pleasure, *he*, they pointed. He lets us sit under the shade but we pay for it, six pounds of my flesh he has torn off. A man pointed to his arm.

But they were shadow grey bent shadows and they moaned in death chants. When we die another will take our stools, our glasses, our plates.

Others will use the john.

Others will laugh and sing and pay.

Six pounds stolen from me.

A cuckoo clock fell from the sky.

Time, time, gentlemen and ladies.

Look.

Oh God he comes again.

No more from my body.

When Ginger stood he saw his wings, felt his beaked nose.

Vulture, vulture, but the shadows fled and all that was on the ground was the smashed clock, he smelled it and flew back to the tree and waited. They have to come. Where else can they go?

"D-23-65"

MACKEY

Lights danced back into Ginger's eyes and teased. What now, what do you wish, please tell us.

Just get the hell out of my field of vision.

Beers four, only bottled; two manhattans, two martinis; do you, kind sir, do you keep your cherries soaked in brandy? No, then take back the manhattan.

Shit, society stinks.

Simon climbing on the wall, speaking matter of factly, There is no such thing as friend as woman or man, we are only beasts who suck each other off. Simon dissolved back into the wall and only the echoes of his voice remained faint but still clear.

Mother Goose, Ryan called; now there was a mother to end all mothers. I could tell you stories of her devotion to family, her lust for the milkman, her cruelty to the butcher and her great charity work.

I could tell you of Humpty Dumpty who rolled drunks and gave the cash to Jill.

Why come? Disrupt another place.

Why come? Disrupt another place. Why come? I came to save my light bill, to let my public see me, to let beautiful girls fuck me, fill them with child. This is my piss hall, my assembly hall, I grant audience here.

Not another drink here.

Pshew, I'll go up the street and get twenty per cent discount. Pshew, I'll go to the candy store a block farther and eat chocolate covered raspberry rolls, you fool.

Edgar, nude in front of him.

Huh?

Where else? My place is cold, you have heat.

There is a charge for heat.

Let me put on my pants and I'll get out.

Now.

You dirty rat.

Beat it, bum, or pay the sum.

How please?

Out.

It's freezing.

The sum, write to mom.

The Palace is my place, all off.

Marjorie and Olivia were engaged in an animated, giggly conversation. Edgar and Ryan were silent, sipping champagne; Ginger stared, they seemed unaware of him. He pinched himself, he wondered how nice he really was, then he sat down and told them the damn dream.

Ryan smiled, You are indeed a complex man, very close to me. Right, Edgar?

Right, but not letting me put my pants on, Joseph—that is the end.

Your end, boy.

Marjorie sighed, It's a wish fulfillment dream. I don't know what that means but you hate us.

Olivia said, You really want to be alone, Mr. Ginger.

You mean have a bar and then let no one go there?

Right, just you and that Palace blazoned in firecrackers outside.

What do you think of the name? Ginger asked carefully.

There's nothing great about the Pines—the name, I mean.

Palace is a more lyrical name; you planning to change it?

You should, Ryan added quickly, you know that theory of mine, names should be changed every few years for no other reason than to elude the police. What's in a name?

No kidding, Ginger said, I been thinking about it.

Sure, Joseph, do it. It's like moving furniture around in a house, everything seems different but it ain't, the room either looks smaller or bigger. You know, change for change's sake. Hell, do it tonight.

The Palace, Edgar mouthed; I like it too.

Ryan said, It would symbolize the type of establishment I could take my daughter to once she has learned to walk and hold her liquor.

Edgar asked, Would you come, Olivia?

She nodded.

Marjorie said, Palace sounds old fashioned, good and secure.

Ginger rubbed his hands, Maybe Sadie won't go for it, she don't like changes.

Ryan patted his back. You tell Sadie she will be the queen of the Palace. You can't miss.

Ryan slapped his hands together, Well, men, that's that.

You want to leave? Marjorie asked.

No, he said. Well, it's not a bad idea, but I didn't mean that. I mean it's the end of something when he changes the name.

But Ryan, you told him to, you encouraged him.

I know, he should do it.

Edgar laughed. Don't get sad-eyed, Ryan.

Don't worry, but when there's a change everything stops for a split second, then of course everything pushes on.

Which way?

It doesn't matter, I just mean it's the end of a time.

You are sad, Marjorie said softly, you're really sad.

Yeah I am. Ginger is too, I bet.

Olivia bit her nails and waited.

The bar is restless, the floor needs waxing, the chair legs are hurting, the tables are tired of being leaned on. Ryan smiled. If I was a wino I might cry.

Edgar rose, Simon had interrupted his first toast but everyone was quiet now, OFF WITH THE OLD, ON WITH THE NEW, THE PINES IS DEAD, LONG LIVE THE PINES.

Marjorie and Olivia smiled but they did not drink. Ryan rose and aiming his empty glass at Ginger who was talking to a bearded customer, Amen and hello PALACE. Ryan held the glass to his ear, Hello PALACE. He tried again louder now. Hello, hello PALACE.

THE MILL

TOM WEATHERS, JR.

It was hot. The mill occupied the earth like an animal in the heat of the sun and around the mill the row upon row of frame dwellings were like small beasts in the presence of a large and dominant beast.

Rafe Jones lived in one of the little houses that was in sight of the mill. He could hear the low whine of the spinning frame from the bedroom where he rested and the sound he heard was always with him, during the night, and during the day.

He lay on the bed and waited for the whistle to blow. When it blew then he would know that he had ten minutes in which to get ready for work.

All about him, throughout the village, more men waited as he did, sweating, not sleeping, in the hot afternoon, and listening for the whistle to signal the start of the second shift.

They were on beds with sheets wet from sweat, and askew from tossing, lying inside the houses that surrounded the mill, separated from one another by dusty strips of hard-packed clay, and broken tricycles, and old cars like dismembered beetles, and trees hanging limply in the heat.

Then from out of the factory, reinforcing the noise of the machines in its bowels there came the strident sound of the whistle. It pierced over the hamlet, into the houses, into the several stores, and it even penetrated into the patriarch-like estate on the hill, sounding soft and eerie there, a reminder in the distance.

When Rafe heard the whistle he opened his eyes and stared without seeing at the wall. Then he brought his vision into focus and got out of the bed. He went to the dresser, and from under a magazine with a picture of a movie actress on its cover, he took out his billfold, a small, well-sharpened knife and some loose change. He put these things in his pockets and stood before the mirror for a moment, looking past the pictures his wife had pasted there, to see himself.

He was not old, nor was he young. The face reflected in the mirror had nothing in it. It was blank. He turned from the mirror and went into the living room.

He was alone. His wife was not at home because she worked the first shift, and their child was not there either. He had gone somewhere and no noise muffled the hollow echo of Rafe's footsteps.

He went to the screen door. It had a patch of cotton stuck in it to keep away the flies, but the cotton did not work and the flies came inside anyway to drone from room to room. Rafe did not care, and he walked out of the door and onto the porch. All around the mill and along the street, in a number of the quiet houses, other men did the same thing.

They stood on the paint flaked and warped wood of their identical porches, then they descended the creaking steps to walk past wilted flowers planted in halves of old tire carcasses, and in the tires filled with dirt, to gather in an ant-like procession in the street.

The men were mostly pale and white-skinned, and they blinked in the harsh light. They were silent. The children that played in the dirt alongside the road, did not pause or look up when a group of the men went by. Rafe's child was playing somewhere like those he passed and he saw the blond head of a boy he thought was his, kneeling in a circle of other boys who were taking turns throwing a knife at a stick. Rafe started to say something but when he came closer he did not recognize the child and he remained silent.

The quiet gathering walked on. In their wake the red dirt of the road was broken into small clouds of dust that hung in the air for a moment then fell.

When they arrived at the mill it was 2:00 p.m. and the men, except Rafe, did not hesitate but walked directly inside. Near the door a tree had once grown to provide an area of shade and transition between the harsh outdoor light and the interior gloom, but the tree had been cut down to give the mill parking space. Rafe stood for a moment and looked at the naked place where the tree had been. Then he joined the others and they disappeared as a group into the dim light of the plant.

The men and women who worked the first shift were waiting for them. They stood by their machines and looked between the door leading into the work area and the old fly-specked clock which hung at a crooked angle on the wall.

Rafe was the last to enter. The light had changed and he blinked his eyes as he walked, not able to see, but with assurance from long travel, to the spinning frame that he operated.

He said hello to the man he was to relieve. The other smiled but except for that his face was as empty as Rafe's. They talked for a while, shouting over the roar of the machines into each other's ears about the work that had been done and the work that was yet unfinished, then the man who had been there during the first shift, left, and Rafe was alone.

He began to do his job, tending the spinning frame with sure and deft movements, his hands of their own volition taking off and replacing bobbins of yarn. His eyes were blank and he walked in a waking dream. No one of the newly arrived crew spoke, and the only noises heard were the ever-present powerful hum of the spinning frame and the loom's furious clatter. The men worked on unceasing and they appeared only as moving shapes, black in the dust and gloom.

After three hours had passed, the people were allowed to go in small groups to the break area. It was located in a corner where there were no windows. On the crates which were used as seats, some of the women had placed old cushions of faded and worn fabric.

Rafe rested on one of these. Beside him sat the woman, Reba. It was not uncommon for men and women on the second and third shifts to have affairs, and Rafe had once been very much involved with Reba. It had died away when she became attracted to another man, but Rafe still had strong feelings for her.

Sitting with her, his eyes were not blank. They looked fiercely at the woman who was made uncomfortable by his gaze. When she rose to leave, Rafe's claw-like hand held her in a tight grip, and she sat down nursing the bruises he had made on her arm.

They did not speak. The woman was nervous and looked away, like a bird, from one place to the other, and her bird-like, high-lifted bosom rose and fell in heavy movements.

Rafe's face burned and his hand shook. He looked at his hand and he looked at the woman: at her thighs, at her buttocks. He held his hand before his face, then he put the still shaking hand on Reba's leg.

She stiffened and screamed, "You're crazy, Rafe. Let me go!"

She tried to move, but he continued squeezing through her work clothes into the yielding rubber flesh of her leg. She screamed again, and one of the other men came to where they were. It was the one that now held the favors of Reba.

He was young and his greasy hair was long. The faded denim pants he wore were tight and his genitals bulged at his crotch.

Rafe did not look at him, nor did he release his grasp on Reba's leg until the man spoke.

"Rafe, goddamn you, let her go!"

Then Rafe stiffened and his eyes grew as blank as they had been before. He looked up. His face was drawn mask-tight as he rose in a slow movement from the crate where he had been sitting, to stand before the man.

Very slowly, very easily, Rafe reached into his pocket and pulled out his knife. He opened it, holding it before his body. Overhead the stained light from a flickering bulb was intensified in harsh gleams reflected from the blade. The other man saw the knife, and when he did, he bent down in a graceful movement to pick up a soft drink bottle, breaking it against the wall, leaving a sharp and jagged nub of glass in his hand.

No word was spoken as the two men walked toward one another. Reba's eyes were bright, and her breath came in heavy, panting sighs. Rafe swung in an arc with his knife, and the other caught him in the face with the broken bottle. There was a flurry of red movement, as violent as the outside afternoon was still, then the two men fell apart, both of them mangled and butchered, to drop bleeding on the floor.

An hour or so later that afternoon, in Asia, an American and a Communist soldier, for no apparent reason began fighting and killed one another. The next morning a similar fight occurred between two parties of fifty men each. In a week's time the world was at war, then after that it was quiet again.

AN INVITATION

TO SEND IN YOUR RESPONSE. RED CLAY READER will be happy to hear your opinions of the book and to forward your comments to the writers you indicate.

TO ENCOURAGE AND SUPPORT the South's literary tradition.

TO GET YOUR COPIES of the RED CLAY READER.

☐ Please send me .... copies of RED CLAY READER for which I enclose $3.00 each (add 9¢ for N. C. sales tax).

☐ Yes, I would like to help establish a major literary market in the South and enclose my patron contribution (tax deductible) of $5.00 or more which will entitle me to a signed copy of the next issue of the RED CLAY READER.

☐ Please send gift copies ($3.00 each or $5.00 for signed first editions) to those persons listed below: **or use this space for your response to RED CLAY READER.**

Name _____

Address _____

City _____ State _____ Zip _____

MAUD F. GATEWOOD

Crone

Espionage—Wien

MAUD F. GATEWOO

MAUD F. GATEWOOD

Hochsatzengasse 6

Opera Coffehouse

Stadtbahn Stop

enna—Incident in the 10th District

AUD F. GATEWOOD

painting with two balls 1960 j. johns

IN PROGRESS...

Besides the million other things that a novel is, it is also a game between the novelist and his audience. For one important element in the novel is surprise; the novelist must keep at least two jumps ahead of his reader, and if the reader "catches" him, if he anticipates turns of character and event with a high degree of accuracy, the jig is up. Boredom sets in quick and hard. And surely in our time only the overblown underbaked long novel called the "best seller" tries successfully to pander to the contemporary addiction to boredom, tries consistently to follow our modern dictum: *Make it look new, that which is as old as the practice of planting corn.* It is the serious novel and the earnest detective story which try, often unsuccessfully, to follow that cleaner, infinitely more difficult axiom of Ezra Pound, actually to *Make it new!*

And in this little game of black and white, in this contest between writer and reader, the writer is necessarily at a disadvantage; the rules he must follow are stringent and it's the reader who holds the foul whistle in his hand, can blow it at any moment. For the surprises in a novel aren't like the surprises in a Christmas package; they can't be just anything. The novelist must intimate, foreshadow, interpret, reinterpret, because it is by these menas that he establishes the belief of his reader in whatever surprise he has in store for him. Every single turn of event or character in a novel must be implicit in any single random page of the book. The reader should know everything that will happen, but without knowing that he knows. The writer must blaze a clear trail to and from every event, and at the same time he must cover his tracks. Even the well-made detective story is exempt from these requirements, which is what makes it—if of course you have the knack—easier to write than the serious novel.

Except that the rules aren't all that easy for the reader either—if he wants any fun out of the game. If he's going to try to guess what will happen in the book (and if he doesn't try the writer has already lost the game), he must read the page, every page, as hard as if it were a letter from a distant, and reticent, lover. Which is, in a way, exactly what a page from a novel is. And in trying to find out what the writer doesn't want him to know yet, he ought to find out most of what the writer does want him to know. Knowing what the writer wants you to know, isn't that the hardest part of reading a book? Reading Mann's *The Magic Mountain* I wonder why the recurrence of the number seven is so goddam important. Does Mann want me to notice it? Why? In Calder Willingham's *End as a Man* is the word "eek" spelled backward really the bloody "key" to the book? Obviously there are a few things that a writer doesn't want you *ever* to know. And maybe this is one of the final gambits which make a novel truly serious, truly a work of art.—At any rate, it should be apparent that novel-reading isn't passive, isn't a spectator sport.

All these considerations, it seems to me, make exciting a selection of episodes from works in progress. These novels really are in progress; while you read this page each of these writers is somewhere chewing his nails for an adjective or verb. You, hapless, are transported into the crazy foul heart of the novelist's workshop, and you have a chance to second guess the poor guy while he is still first guessing. If you read with a hard eye, listen with a sensible ear, you may be able to intuit his whole book before he gets it down, or maybe you can intuit a better book than he will actually write. If the latter case obtains, maybe it's time you began sharpening pencils yourself. But hopefully neither of these alternatives is true, hopefully there are surprises on these pages that you can't see yet, things big and sweet and simple, yet as invisible and as powerful as love. And surely you won't be satisfied with intimations, with hints, you will want to *know*, and when these books appear whole you will want to read them. I would, if only to see if I was as smart as I'd thought. For myself, I find the prospects glimpsed in these pages quite simply exhilarating.

FRED CHAPPELL

FRAGMENT FROM DAGON BY FRED CHAPPELL

When Peter woke his gangly frame was shuddering all over, not just from the morning cool, but because this was the condition of his awaking body. He struggled with his limbs. The chains clashed and thumped on the splintery floor. He didn't want to open his eyes. The early sunlight would strike like a bullet into his brain. The smell of slopped liquor, of chewed rancid scraps of food, hung in the room, only slightly freshened by the raw air that poured in. A window was broken or maybe somebody had left the door open. The light was on his eyelids, forming behind them a coarse abrasive red curtain which made his temples ache. An uncontrollable belch brought up the whole fetor of his gut and while he struggled to breathe, keeping his mouth open to dissipate the deathly taste, droplets of sweat popped out over his whole length, dampening his shirt and pants which were already salty and sour from the weeks before. He gasped.

Then he lay still, trying to listen, but all he could hear was his own thick choked breathing. When he held his breath he could hear only the blood swarming in his ears. But no one seemed to be awake but himself; he had to lie still. If he woke them, moving his chains loud enough to wake them, they would kick him to bits. He tried to place his head, without moving his arms and legs, so that the sun couldn't get at his eyes. It was no good. The day had already begun its dreadful course, the sun was poisoning the sky. He felt the baleful rays sink into his pores. His spine felt as if metallic cold hands squeezed it intermittently. He couldn't get his face out of the sunlight.

He lapsed into a fitful red doze, but was jarred awake by the fear of rattling the chains in his sleep. With her big mouth Mina would tear his Adam's apple out of his throat. She would spit it on the floor and crush it with her big mean heel, like killing a cockroach. He could almost see her unmoving face hovering over his, feel the cold fishy breath of her; her teeth would be like hundreds of relentless needles. He whimpered helplessly, but stopped it off, constricting his throat like a ball of iron inside. If he began whimpering hard he couldn't stop and it would get louder and louder until the moos came on him,

and then they would beat him until he stopped. He stopped the whimper. His chest already felt jagged inside where they had kicked him. He fought to make all his muscles relax from the quivering, and stream on stream of tears rolled down his face. If he opened his eyes the tears would shoot sharp spears through them.

But he was so tired he was almost inanimate. He fell into a yellow sleep, bitter with a drilling electric sound and the smell of black mud and fish. He dreamed that he had no face at all and that his eyes were unseeing dark splotches on his gray stony back and that he swam forever through this world of solid objects which were to his body liquid. In the dream there was nothing he could touch, his body was mere extension without knowable presence.

Again he came awake, now with the black thirst upon him. The sunlight no longer filled his face, and yet he did not think that he had slept long. He felt a warm presence. At first his eyes wouldn't open, and he thought that they had clicked them shut forever with locks and he thrashed around, beginning to whimper again, not caring about the chains now. He got his eyes open, though they were still unseeing, but it was hard to breathe. He blew his breath out hard and an inexplicable chicken feather blew up and stuck on his cheek. He gagged. Then when he could look it was all dim, but behind the dimness was a bright white ball with the hurt strained out of it.

He could not think any more. Everything in his head was gone. At last he realized he was looking at the sun. It shone through the dark gray cloth, reddening faintly the stretched muscles of the legs which arched over his face. He knew them already, Mina's plump steady legs, taut curve at calf and thigh, arrogant, careless. He looked up the pink-tinged insides of her legs. He knew he had always been right. There at the X of her where her woman-thing ought to be was a spider as big as a hand, furred over with stiff belligerent hairs straight as spikes. He couldn't stop looking. His gullet closed and his chest began to strain for air; he could hear it begin to crackle. His throat opened again, but it was hard to breathe because the whimpering had started. It started loud and he knew there was no hope stopping. The moos had got to come now; and then they would kick him to bits.

"Hush up, just hush up," she said. "Can't you never take a joke?" With the hand which wasn't holding up the front of her skirt she reached down there and plucked the spider away. She held it free above him and though he could see it was only a toy, only wire and fuzz and springy legs, he couldn't keep the whimpering back. It got louder; the moos had got to come.

She dropped her skirt and leaned her face over him, rolling it a little so that he could see she was disgusted. "Well there, then," she said. She shook the toy spider in her hand and then dropped it on his face.

He tried not to, he clenched his teeth and tried to keep it back, but the noiseless loud fear poured out of his mouth, moo after moo of it, pure craziness. He was so frightened he couldn't hear himself, and he heard Mina calling:

"Coke! Coke! Come in here right now. Come in here."

Before she had stopped shouting the watery blond boy came in. He didn't even look at Mina but simply put the heel of his boot on Peter's chest and ground his foot round and round, pushing down hard. The blond boy pushed harder until Peter couldn't breathe any more, and he had to stop mooing. Then the boy squatted and sat on his chest, bouncing his weight up and down so that he couldn't get out his fear. He drummed his arms and legs, banging the chain links, rubbing them across the floor.

The blond boy began to slap his face first with one hand and then with the other. "What's my name?" he said.

"Coke."

He slapped him again and again. "What's the rest of it? What's my full name?"

Peter was cold with unknowing. He formed sounds but no name emerged from them.

"Come on, baby. Stick with it. What's my full name, now?" The slapping had got progressively harder.

"Coke Rymer," he said.

"*That's* my baby," the blond boy said in a soothing tone of voice. "That's a way to go." He stood up with the meaningless nonchalance he always had about him. "We'll get you a drink now, okay?" Without pausing for an answer he kicked Peter hard on the side of his neck. "That's a baby," he said.

He groaned at the kick, but after the first uttering of pain was out he subsided into the whimpering which finally became only a strained silent heaving of his chest. He kept looking up at Coke's liquescent blue gaze; his own eyes were charged with pain and fear but not with hate. He would never have any more hate.

Apparently satisfied, Coke Rymer knelt and began to unlock the chained cuffs at his wrists and ankles.

He was still murmuring soothingly. "All right now, you're coming right along. You're going to do all right, honey, you're going to do all *right*." When he finished with the locks he handed the bunch of keys on the long chain to Mina. She dropped the chain loop over her head, tucked the keys into her cotton blouse and buttoned it up. She stood away from the two of them, her arms folded. Coke Rymer hoisted him to his feet and held him up until he seemed steady enough to stand by himself. He stood wavering, his head dropped almost to his chest and lolling back and forth; floundered across the room and leaned backward against the flimsy dinette table. He stroked carefully at his wrists; there were scarlet ichorous bands on them where the broad iron cuffs had rubbed the skin away. It made him feel very pitying to see his poor wrists like this.

"Huh," Mina said. "You ain't hurt. That's nothing."

"We'll get him a drink of liquor," Coke Rymer said. "That'll fix our little honeybunch up before you know it. Make a new man out of him." He swung open one of the rickety wall cupboard doors. Inside it was full of empty bottles and broken glass. He brought down a pint bottle of murky stuff and shook it, looked at it against the broad light that streamed through the open door. "What'll you give me for this?" he said. He showed his dim little teeth in a stretched smile.

He could barely grunt. It sounded like gravel rattling in a box.

"Oh, go on and give it to him," Mina said. She watched him patiently, as if she was curious. Of course curiosity would never show in that locked face.

The boy held it out to him and he waited a wary moment to see if it would be jerked away. He got hold of it in both hands and then again momentarily just stood clutching it out of fear of dropping or spilling it. He drank in short convulsive swallows. It tasted thick and mushy and warm but it had a burning around the edges. As he lowered the bottle he lowered his head too and then again he stood clenching the bottle and, with the muscles of his chest, clenching his insides too. He had to keep it down, couldn't let it get away from him; he stood taut from his heels to his chin. After a long time the writhing spasms stopped. Again sweat came out on him all over.

Mina was still watching him. She spoke in an observing even tone: "They's chicken blood in that liquor."

He was still stuporous; her face was as blank to him as paper.

"You was the one done it, yourself," she said. "You was the one pulled that chicken's head off and crammed that neck down in the bottle. I guess you didn't know it, but that's what you done. It was just last night." In the morning sunlight her eyes seemed whiter than ever.

Coke Rymer sniggered.

He looked clumsily at the bottle in his hands, then put it carefully on the table. He was a long way past caring now. He stood still, waiting and dazed.

She stirred her feet and began talking to the blond boy. She had the full relaxed air of someone who has just seen a difficult juggling trick performed successfully. "Me and the girls has got to go off," she said. "I got to get me something to wear for tonight. You better keep your eye on him good while we're gone and see he gets this place cleaned up some. Don't let him drink too much of that liquor so he can't do nothing. You better get him something to eat at dinnertime too. We got to make him eat something."

His mind was clearing some. The narrow avenues of what he knew of his labors and his fear had emerged a little from the wet smoke. He understood that she was talking about him but that he didn't have to listen. And then he had to. She was telling him something. "Go on in there and wake them girls up," she said. "We got to get going."

"Wait a minute," Coke Rymer said. He turned to her. "I want to show him something." He came across to where Peter stood and spread his hand flat on the table, his fingers wide apart. "Look here," he said, "I want to show you something." He fetched a big folded knife from his pocket and let it roll in his hand. When he moved his thumb a sharp crying blade jumped from his fist, circled in the air. Peter moved back a little, trembling. The knife was Coke Rymer's manthing, he didn't want it to hurt him; he didn't want to see it. Coke Rymer laid it on the table and twirled it around with his index finger. He was giggling. He picked the knife up at the end of the blade, pinching it with his thumb and forefinger. "Look at this," he said. He hesitated and then flipped the knife quickly upward. It spun round and round, a flashing pinwheel. When it came down the blade chucked into the tabletop in the space between the third and fourth fingers of Coke Rymer's left hand. He giggled. The knife quivered to stillness.

"That's enough of that stuff now," Mina said. "I want him to get some things done today. I don't want you messing around and playing with him all the time. He's got to get some things done."

Coke Rymer folded the knife and put it away. He turned toward her. "You want me to hide that ole pump handle?"

"I reckon not. You just quit deviling him and leave him alone. He's enough trouble the way he is already, without you picking at him."

"I wasn't hurting him none."

"Just leave him alone, I said." She spoke to Peter. "I thought I told you already to get them girls out of bed. I ain't got all day to fool around with you."

He slouched forward, going reluctantly toward the bedroom. He wanted her to make sure the yellow-haired boy wouldn't disturb the pump handle; she ought to stop him. The pump handle solaced him with its length and its fine heaviness in his hand; he loved to stroke along the long subtle curve of it; he liked

just to have it near him, to hold it out before himself, admiring its blazing shininess and its heft. Hours and hours he had spent scrubbing and shining and oiling it. He knew that Mina derived a clear satisfaction from knowing that it was his man-thing, and he thought she ought not let Coke Rymer dally with it.—He couldn't understand the blond boy. There was nothing in him, nothing at all; he didn't understand why Mina tolerated him.

He lumbered through the narrow doorway into the living room. In here the light was dimmer and didn't bulge in his head so much. The torn shade was pulled almost down in the north window; little chinks and blocks of light shone in the holes. Through the west window he could see the squat cheap white frame house across the street, all yellow in the sunlight. One pillow lay staggered on the floor, dropped from the springs of the stained greasy wine-colored sofa across the room; along the top of the sofa back all the prickly nap had worn away. On the black little end table was the radio, which was on—the radio was always on, but now nobody had bothered to tune it to a station and it uttered only staccato driblets of static. There were a couple of broken cardboard boxes in one corner of the room, and a few sheets of newspaper were scattered on the floor. On the east wall next the window were dime store photographs of Marilyn Monroe, Jayne Mansfield and Elvis Presley, all dotted with flyshit. At the edge of the sofa and in two corners of the room were blurred remnants of the pattern which had once covered the dull rubbed linoleum.

The bedroom was to the left of the livingroom and he entered without knocking. A dark green shade covered the single bedroom window and in here it was much dimmer than in the livingroom. He had to wait until his eyes adjusted to the darkness. Heaped together in the small bed in the corner—the big double bed on the left was Mina's—the girls stirred restlessly, sensing in their sleep Peter's presence in the room. He went to the bed, grasped a protruding pale shoulder and shook it as gently as he could. The startled flesh moved under his nerveless hand. "Whah." He shook her again and she mumbled some more and sat up. Because of the dimness her sharp face looked detached, a soft lantern. It was Bella. Her black hair came forward, hiding her face; she shook her head, raised her arms and stroked her hair back over her shoulders. Only her face and her breasts stood visible. Her breasts were like featureless faces; they bobbed softly as she fixed her hair. Enid shifted in her sleep, turning toward them, and flung her thin arm over Bella's gentle belly. She stopped manipulating her hair and for a moment stroked carefully the arm which lay on her.—He knew that this too was one of Mina's satisfactions, that Bella and Enid were after the woman in each other.—Then she tapped Enid's arm. "Sweetheart," she said, her voice thick and throaty from sleep, "wake up. Mina must want us to get up. Come on." Enid dug deeper into the bed.

Bella looked up at him, her gaze abstracted, visionless. Momentarily it seemed to him that there was something she wanted from him, and the thought frightened him. He stumbled back from the bedside.

"What do you think you're doing?" she said. Her voice was regaining its natural sharpness. "Go on away. Go get where you belong."

As he went out the door he saw Bella resume her loving ministering to Enid.

Mina was talking to Coke Rymer in the livingroom, and Peter went straight through and straight through the kitchen out to the back porch. He wanted to check his pump handle, to see if it was still where he had hidden it—that was the one thing he could remember from the day before. The porch cracked and swayed under his footsteps, the boards weakening with rot or termites. A double handful of big blue and green flies were flocked on the carcass of the headless chicken that lay there. They skipped about on the queasy body, making a noise like muttered swearing. Already the air was hot, viscid, and the singing of the flies seemed to increase the oppressiveness of the heat. He nudged the chicken with his bare toe and the flies swirled up in a funnel-shaped pattern and then settled again immediately. With his forearm he wiped his mouth; he couldn't understand how he could do something like that. All the glare of the sun seemed focused on the murdered bird.

He stepped down into the fluffy dust of the back yard. The yard was small and underneath the dust was burning packed clay. A ruptured hog wire fence unevenly straggled the rectangular borders, and here and there long shoots of blackberry vine poked through. In the north corner of the yard was the little low weatherstained shed from which he averted his eyes without even thinking about it, with the strength of a habit enforced by sheer instinct. He went around the edge of the little porch, which was laid out at the back of the house like a perfunctory throw rug, and peeked underneath it, where the pile of daubed stones supported it. There, crosswise in a space between two joists, lay the pump handle. He hadn't realized until

he found the handle that he'd been holding his breath and it came in a swoop out his mouth and nose, all too heavily redolent of what had happened to his insides. He wiped his mouth. He got the pump handle and stood and held it before him, hefting it warm and solid in his hand, beholding it in the sunlight. He examined it all over for a speck of rust or dirt, but it was clean and shiny as quicksilver.

"Well, so that's where you keep it, then? Well, that's all I wanted to know."

He looked up. Coke Rymer was standing at the edge of the porch, leaning against the post support and whittling slowly at the edge of it. Dismayed, Peter stepped back.

Coke Rymer showed his meaningless grin; his teeth were little and yellow. "That's all in the world I needed to know, where you keep hiding that ole pump handle."

He stepped farther back, gingerly swinging the bright handle like a pendulum in front of his legs. He decided that if the wavery blond boy got down into the yard after him he would hit him, he would make blood come. Already now he was whimpering.

The other folded his knife and returned it to his pocket. "Aw, hush up. I ain't going to hurt you." He grinned again. "You better come on in here now and get started on this stuff Mina wants you to get done. She's liable to get mad if you don't, and I guess you don't want her to get mad at you. You'd be a even more pitiful sight than you are if she was to get mad and get a hold of you."

Still he hung back, but he had stopped swinging the pump handle. He clasped it fondly across his belly.

Coke Rymer looked at him. "Aw, you can bring that old thing with you. What's it matter to me?" He turned and briskly went inside.

He shuffled unsteadily up the two creaky steps, onto the porch. He didn't mind the work so much. He was just hoping they wouldn't make him eat the gooey soft-fried eggs and toast for lunch.

FROM **DOWERIES** BY RICHARD GOLDHURST

There is a Charlotte, North Carolina, a Westport, Connecticut, and a New York City, but the author is not sure real people in any of these places have ever committed adultery.

"Is Orville out on night patrol?" asked Felix Bonnerstein, slipping into the booth beside Mrs. Armogene Summerfield.

"No," she said, blinking her green-blue eyes. "Tonight's the Mother-Son Bowling Tournament at the

Coliseum Bowling Alley. Orville and Mama Summerfield are going to win it."

"You mean nobody's out at your house now?"

"I'm going to be there soon," she said.

"Let's go out there, you and me. He and his mother will be gone quite a while, won't they?"

"Felix Bonnerstein," she asked, "whut are you suggesting?"

"The same thing I suggest when we go to motels at noon."

"Orville likes bowling better'n anything," she said. "I just think it would be terribly risky."

"How can he be so goofy about bowling married to a girl like you?" asked Felix.

"You mean if you were married to me you'd give up bowling?"

"Listen, honey," said Felix, "if I were married to you I'd give up Elizabeth Taylor."

"Felix, why can't you get a separate apartment? We could go there noontimes and evenings instead of all those motels where we have to make up names."

"Because if I didn't live at home I wouldn't be able to pay my wife three hundred and fifty dollars a month like the judge ordered me to. As it is, the motels are putting me in hock. Now come on, what do you say? Let's go to your house."

There were several reasons why Armogene finally consented to so risky and foolish an assignation. One of the reasons she consented was precisely because it was risky and foolish. She was under the impression only love led men to risky and foolish proposals. Most Americans find true love akin to panic and Armogene Atkins Summerfield was no exception. She was an American girl compelled to fulfill the demands of love to satisfy her romantic conception of herself. She also consented because she was sure there was every chance she would get away with it tonight.

Armogene was a native of Danville, Virginia, where her father had been the assistant superintendent of schools. During the Depression, part of her father's salary had been the coal with which he heated his house. Armogene was the only girl on the block who didn't smell of kerosene. Things like that make a woman feel she's precious.

She went to the Danville Business College and just about the time she mastered the intricacies of the Pittman system she met Orville Summerfield, then a student at VMI. The first thing he told her about himself was that he was one-eighth Lumbee Indian. Being one-eighth Indian was one of the central facts about Orville's existence. He had, however, none of the vices

"THURBER'S OWL WHO WAS GOD"

of the Indian: he didn't whoop when he got drunk, he wasn't close-mouthed, and he didn't treat all women like squaws—he knew, for instance, there was a difference between a college girl like Armogene who went to the Danville Business College and the flirts who populated the local Howard Johnson's. She said yes when he asked her to marry him, thinking it would be a marvelous middle-age to be the wife of a general who was one-eighth Lumbee Indian and to live on an Army post where no one reeked of kerosene.

What she didn't understand about Orville was that he was at VMI because he had an inordinate love of uniforms. In fact, when that venerable institution refused to award him a commission because of his inferior grades, he was just as happy when the Charlotte, North Carolina, Police Force took him on as a probationary motorcycle cop and issued him blue jodphurs with a yellow band down the leg, a white shirt, black boots, and a shiny plastic helmet with goggles.

Though he had never met Orville Summerfield, and had no wish to, Felix understood that the man's passion for uniforms and his Indian blood helped make Armogene an adulteress. Every time Armogene looked at that closet full of uniforms, the black shiny boots

sticking up like Paris chimneys, she wondered what had taken her from the sanctity of the Danville Business College to Charlotte, North Carolina, and the dreary rounds of entertaining and being entertained by policemen's wives. The only activity at which Orville excelled was bowling. Orville arranged the loving cups he won with the same pride previous Lumbee Indians felt hanging scalps in the tepees. She consented to Felix Bonnerstein because he was Jewish and a city hall reporter and because he never bored her talking about how much he had paid in toward his pension.

Armogene lived quite a distance out from Charlotte, in Montclair, where all the houses lined up as neatly and symmetrically as crosses in a military graveyard. She parked in her driveway and saw Felix, following her, drive on to the bottom of the hill, make

A. HILL

a U-turn and come back. In front of her house, he left his motor idling. No one suspects anything of a male visitor who leaves his motor idling.

The Summerfield residence was one of those bastardized houses ignorant contractors throw up for the benefit of talkative realtors. The living room promised neither comfort nor warmth. The hearth was disadvantageously placed too near the door. The kitchen was topheavy with steel cabinets. It barely accommodated a dining table. A picture window sighted on the neighbor's weeds.

Armogene was already down the hall and Felix followed her into a miniature den outfitted with a television set, a couch, a small typing table and typewriter. On the brick wall, where the rest of Montclair's residents hung driftwood, was the house's supreme distinction: a Lumbee war bonnet. Crisscrossing below were two long peace pipes. Without asking, Felix understood why Armogene had chosen this room. She had an innate delicacy. She didn't want to make love on the master bed.

"Oh," she said, "this is going to make me so nervous."

"It's not something we haven't done before," said Felix.

"But is it fair to Orville?"

"If you want an honest answer," said Felix, "no." He put his arm around her waist and tried waltzing her to the couch.

"Felix," she asked breathlessly, "you *are* going to be a great Jewish syndicated columnist, aren't you?"

"Certainly," said Felix, trying to kiss her ear. She wouldn't betray Orville with another cop, he thought, not even J. Edgar Hoover, but a Washington correspondent was something else.

"Let me pull down these blinds," she said, squirming from his grasp. At the window she became a statue, absolutely still, her hand frozen on the venetian blind's release cord.

"That car," she said in a weak voice which nevertheless perfectly communicated emergency, "that car coming up the road looks just like Orville's."

"How could it be Orville?" asked Felix nonchalantly. "He and his mother couldn't have bowled the qualifying frames yet let alone win the tournament."

Her voice rasped like dry chalk on a blackboard. "It is Orville."

"What's he doing here?" asked Felix, sensing perhaps alarm was filling the night.

"My God," said Armogene, "there's Mama Summerfield's bowling ball." She pointed. There, by the desk, was a dappled bowling ball, held snug in its box by a pair of bowling shoes squeezed beside it. "Mama Summerfield forgot her bowling ball. Orville's coming back to get it. Felix, whut're we going to do?"

"Roll the ball out to him," said Felix.

"Run out the back way," she said.

"No good, dear, my car's out front."

"He'll catch us," said Armogene. "He'll catch us. He's getting out of his car now. He's looking at your car."

"If his service revolver's around here," said Felix, "you better unload it."

"He's studying your car and wondering," she said. "He's wondering and wondering. I think he always carries his revolver. I think that's regulations."

Felix moaned.

"He's coming in, Felix," she said. "Felix, *whut* are we going to do?"

"If he shoots me," said Felix, "I suppose you'll have to stick beside him."

"Felix, you better tell me whut we're going to do."

He thought, now it's all my fault. He went to the typing table and picked up the small Smith-Corona portable. He hefted it once and said sharply, "Now, Armogene, I am the typewriter repair man. I have come to pick up your typewriter. The 'e' doesn't strike. The platen is worn. It needs cleaning. Tell me these things at the front door."

She stood rooted.

"Shake your little Danville ass," said Felix and left the room. She followed then. They reached the living room a split second before the bemused Orville came through the front door.

He's got his hand in his pocket on his gun, thought Felix.

"The 'e' on this typewriter doesn't work," fluted Armogene, as persuasive as Sarah Bernhardt. "The platen is worn. It needs cleaning."

"Yeah," said Orville, walking toward them and putting his nose to the typewriter Felix held. "Sometimes when you make all capitals the shift won't release."

Orville was tall and husky with prominent cheekbones protecting his slitted eyes. His hair was straight and dark. More than an Indian, however, Felix thought he looked like a fellow who would flunk out of the Virginia Military Institute.

"We'll fix it," said Felix. "Don't worry about that."

"And the little bell doesn't work, either," said Orville. "Sometimes when I'm typing my traffic reports, I run right off'n the page."

"That can be annoying," said Felix.

"I've been thinking of bringing it in to some repair shop for weeks," Orville continued, "ever since I found out a new one took eighty-five books of S and H trading stamps."

"It needs a new ribbon, too," said Felix.

"Don't forget the platen," said Armogene.

The last thing Felix heard as he pulled the door closed behind him was Orville explaining, "Armogene, I got to get Mama Summerfield's bowling ball. She's already got a terrible blister on her thumb using mine."

FROM
THE CAPTIVITY OF PIXIE SHEDMAN

BY ROMULUS LINNEY

Often in New York I journey through the mountains of North Carolina. Under peaks and stabs of many-leveled apartments, in my bed at night asleep I am disturbed by underground faults, buckling the bedrock granite of Manhattan Island, so that while eons pass in a moment's sleep, so do the towers of this city in a metamorphosis of dream and deep yearning soften, their razor-sharp corner-lines are dulled, flattened, their canopied, store-fronted bases pushed out, the spires, cupolas and flat-topped tenement ranges of uneven heights merge into the great roll and swerve of the Appalachian mountains. Tossing on my bed, I sleep and dream and create the landscapes of childhood out of the stone, light and sullen glare of maturity.

So with a sweep of the Hudson River up along the West Side Drive, I swing my second-hand Plymouth around the corner of a furious thruway, and come not to the George Washington Bridge but to Stand Around, N. C., which is not near Riverdale or Westchester but Dog Slaughter Creek, which is not near Darien or New Haven, but a tiny town once called Virgin's Gap, changed now, and what a pity, to Hidersburg. In my dream I know very well that from Stand Around, in five miles' travel on this back country road, I will come to an intersection of two roads. Both will be crumbling macadam, and now I suppose they are overgrown with weeds, but in the time I dream of they met to form the only highway into these mountains from Tennessee, much traveled in the summer, when on his vacation my father would take his family back for a visit to the small mountain town where he was born.

A flash of Forty-second Street neon, purple hair and pink pedal-pushers, quiet and deadly lounging of dignified, crumbling male whores against cigar-store windows, behind them in fierce diminishing perspective the movie houses with double features for sixty cents, a canvas of frightening human damage and equally frightening immediate human escape, whose bizarre color and strange pulse is reflected in my dream, as for me is all reality, in the rising drive of these mountains. The harshness and the color is much the same. Random spectacles place my grandmother's April flowers on the screen of my car windows, and behind them, gigantic grey-green mountain flanks are heaving to sprout tangles of brazen azealea and chaste white dogwood, spring rains soak down from the wet peaks, gush into cascades of water and mud and loose shale. It is the haphazard flow of so generous an issue that when you drive around a curve a hundred yards away,

even sitting inside the car you feel the cool delight of slope water in the air and wind, delicious. You pass the water-break, which spills down the roadside wall of dripping sandstone, spreading full and strong and straight over the crumbling little macadam road, pushing shale and weed and mud ahead of it. Over the cool flow of an issue of mountains a man may rejoice in the generosities of spring rain, he can think, in this gushing resource of nature, of life again.

So did my father. At the little two-road intersection, he would begin to sing. Even on those last two trips. For from this turning the old Chrysler he drove headed straight into the mountains. There would be no stops from that point on. He drove with a very thoughtful speed, so anxious to get to that mountain town that he handled his automobile carefully as an airplane, which would set us down behind a large house overlooking the main street of a small town, a house that held the secrets of his birth and all the myriad tangles of Shedman past and present, in whose rooms the two Bertrams before my father and myself lived, and on whose porch, though never at one time, all four Bertram Shedmans faced Pixie as grandson, son, husband and father-in-law.

From this intersection, created again in my dreams, my father would begin to sing. From here on, while I shot Indians from the back windows with wonderful childish two-board wooden pistols, he who often hummed and whistled but seldom sang would forget his wife and child and profession, would forget on those last two trips the dark cancer swelling in his throat, and in a hoarse ravaged voice, sing, off-key but merry. My mother had learned to love the moments he could forget even her and me, and she would smile. Down the slopes that fall away from the road more and more steeply the higher you climb, rolled my stricken Indians, knocked into a feathered tumble and a blaze of war and dark skin by the unerring, spurting bullets from my fine two-board wooden gun. We round a curve, I lean out the window and fire at a bored Cherokee Indian who is dressed up to stand in front of a gas station tourist trap, who nods and manages a slight wave of his bow.

Now, dreaming, driving again into the mountains in my own car, I feel behind me another car pushing, wanting ahead. I veer to the side of the road and am passed by the Chrysler sedan. I follow it now, as driven by my father it goes on, slowing down a little by a swift mountain stream that I see him eyeing carefully, leaning his head out of the window a bit, gripping the steering wheel and looking for trout water and casting banks. I follow them going home, as both our cars climb up into the Appalachian mountains, passing the sprawling crumbled barns with faded primary color advertisements for snuff and farm equipment, past the small houses and country stores, past the soft-loamed hills that now are beginning to be topped by soaring, ragged backs of ridges reaching up even higher in the sky finally to fragment, to crumble into water-ribbed, life giving channels of bedrock, and hold, achieved, in the air.

In the car that I follow, my father relaxes his grip on the wheel, feels again a surge of life in the loins of his dying body, and sings. In the back seat, with his tiny wooden gun the little boy shoots anything he sees and points his joyous innocent weapon at the world. With her husband and her son, rising up into the mountains of North Carolina, the woman smiles.

Even though they vanish quickly in a maze of roads, and I am journeying alone now, faced with mountains, I still begin to sing.

From the cluttered apartment up over the unused garage walks Pixie, me stumbling after then running ahead to stop and look back at her as she picks her way with dainty steps, helped by a bronze-tipped umbrella tightly closed and wrapped about with a purple ribbon. She wears a ruffled blouse with square shoulders and a high neck, a long black skirt, tiny patent leather walking shoes with buttons, and she carries a straw lunch basket in one elegantly crooked arm. Pressed against her side is a folded, homespun blanket.

As she walks, her tiny cameo face, pale and delicate, turns idly from side to side, gazing at the weeds, rocks and fence pieces and sheds along this backroad that leads nowhere as if they were all most interesting sights. We pass the last house on the road. It is a great wreck, set back twenty-five yards from the dirt road. Circling it is a wide arena of bare ground, hard-packed dirt, tamped bare by the feet of many children born and running on it year after year, littered by scraps of upturned, rusted machinery, broken toys, oil drums and slashed tin cans. Through this maze wander two mournful, limp-uddered cows. A squawking flight of scrawny chickens skitter about, plagued by a host of children who are throwing rocks at them from the porch of the house.

Just a moment, Bertram.

Pixie crosses her wrists under the handle of the lunch basket, stands holding it with such straight-backed dignity you would think it was a prayerbook.

Hello, Sam.

Hello, Pixie, how are you today?

Just fine. Sam, I have a job for you. Are you free tomorrow?

On the porch stands a man unshaven, slack-chested, squint-eyed. His neck seems as thin and scrawny as those of the chickens, his eyes do not seem quite level with each other in his face, and his lower and upper lips seem to belong to two different people. He stands up slowly from a battered easy chair stuffed with hay and bows to Pixie, with clumsy elaboration. The children stop throwing their rocks, gaze at their father and at Pixie and at me.

Sam, I want to move my bookcases around again. You come by tomorrow morning and I'll put you to work on it. And I need some things done in the

kitchen too, so bring your wrenches and things with you.

Pixie, I'll be glad to help you out any way I can.

Thank you, Sam. Hello, Lena.

Hello, Pixie. How are you today?

Fine. Come along, Bertram.

We leave them, passing the house, and I stare back at the man, who immediately collapses into his hay-stuffed chair, at the children who stare after us, and at the woman who came out onto the porch, who seems to be held up by an invisible hook at the back of her neck, hanging a string of badly jointed bones inside a wrinkled bag that is stained, flopped, knotted and rinsed by child after child after child until now she slumps exhausted, hanging suspended from the hook of a merciless, perhaps appreciative creator, who may be hoping for one or two more children before Lena decides enough, goes to her bed and dies.

Back and forth in Pixie's slow path, ahead of her and behind her, I ask about the dirty children and the lopsided man and the woman who did not stand but hung there on an invisible hook.

Curious, are you, Bertram?

Yes, Pixie. Come on and tell me.

How much will you give me if I tell you?

I hop, jump and calculate quickly.

I'll give you what you pay him for tomorrow that really needs to be done. How's that?

That's pretty good for a ten year old. You're going to be another smart Shedman, Bertram. Another smart Shedman.

The lunch basket prods me along as we move off the road onto a cowpath, climbing now up to the stand of birch trees where Pixie takes me for a picnic each time I visit her. It is summer, hot and verdant. Through the random growth and the heavy summer air her slow and biting words tell Bertram age ten about the frame house, children and exhausted husband and wife, and tell Bertram now aged 24, lying in the bed her death has vacated, with this April Maysville nightwind sweeping across me, about herself.

Which flowers grew where I cannot remember, and certainly along this road, this cowpath and between these birches we do not find them all, all the biology bookful of flowers that in her lifetime passed from my waspish grandmother's hand to mine. And most of the time they were not the real flowers at all, only pictures cut out of horicultural magazines, with the outlandish names under the colorful prints. Nevertheless, I am close to Pixie now through those flowers, as I lie in her tiny dark home after her death, remembering her through White Baneberry, whose stalks redden with age, whose china-white fruit is poisonous and gleams in the shade, and she says, *Yes, you're right, smart Bertram, I do give Sam work that doesn't need to be done. I do pay him money I don't need to. Don't you think that's generous of me, though?* Over the bloodroot poppy we walk, and it is pink as dawn but when it is crushed it gives a scarlet liquid useful as war paint, dye, and it can cause a color change and disguise of an eye. I chant, *Depends on why, Pixie, depends on why. Why do you do it?* Past lank green swaths of wild yam and meadowrue, smirking at me, answering obliquely, *Yes, a smart Shedman already. Well, that old house was your family home once upon a time. I thought you knew that. Maybe you're not so smart, after all. That house was the great center of your famous great grandfather's famous great holdings. His vast land, his wealth, his farm he called Arabia. He had all his children there. Your grandfather was born in that house. And he was the one who sold it. I thought you knew that.*

Past nodding suns of blackeyed Susan, yellow sweetclover, turkscap lilies and fourleaf loosestrife, *Oh yes I knew that, sure I knew that.*

Off the cowpath, walking now through low timothy grass toward the trees, *Did you, now? Well, did you also know you might be visiting me there today if your grandfather hadn't sold his father's house, sold it because he didn't like to think about it? It would have looked now the way it used to, Bertram, if he hadn't done that, sold it away from us.* Solomonplume orange with stems that zigzag and berries green and red all at once, *So why didn't he want to think about it, Pixie? Why did he sell it, was it old and falling down? Why didn't he like it?* Laughter, her stride picking up through the scarlet fireweed and bull thistle and thimbleberry, *Well, he didn't like it for the same reason I now find work for Sam that doesn't need to be done or paid for. Figure that one out if you're such a smart Shedman.* Her laughter now becomes shrill and harsh, her dainty step is rushed over crowpoison and allegany goatsbeard whose brownish blossoms become quickly infested with insects. *Pixie that's not fair. Come on now and tell me why he didn't like it and why you give Sam money, come on now Pixie, you better.* Sighs from her and mysterious chuckles, we have reached the stand of trees and now she looks around from the top of this small hill with the lunch basket in both hands, held like a longago schoolgirl's hat across her legs. She leans back against the linen trunk of a birch tree, grandmother no longer, smiling, saying, *Children, Bertram. Children.*

Children? Children? What do you mean children? I take from her hand the homespun blanket and spread it over all the flowers I remember when I think of her, solomonplume orange and yellow loosestrife, baneberry and fireweed and all the rest. I take off my tennis shoes and flop on the blanket while she hands me the lunch basket to open. *Children because Sam and Lena have so many of them and they have the house too*, standing still, leaning back with her eyes closed, then looking at me sharply when I laugh, and say, *Well, Pixie, I did see that all those children sure but why give him money for that, why money for having children, Pixie?* Through me like a needle into cloth her cold stare, *Why not, Bertram, why not, may I ask?* And now the moment that always comes when I am alone with Pixie for very long, the moment I become afraid of her. I fumble with the lunch box. *Never mind why not, Pixie, come on now I asked you first.*

With a rustle of skirts she seats herself in slow descent onto the blanket. We sit there, riding it over the flowers. She looks into the basket, takes out a white napkin, hands it to me, saying, *They are the same thing because Sam has given his all, Bertram. He's pretty worthless, Sam is, and what else he ever had to give I can't imagine, but that he did give. Fourteen children, and a hard time taking care of any of them. So I help them out. Generous?*

Sure, Pixie, I guess so.

Guess, do you. Is that all?

That cold stare again as I munch a drumstick, good cold chicken now tasteless, lying on my stomach my toes touching the crabgrass at the limits of the blanket, saying, *Why should I know anything about it, why shouldn't I guess?*

Because you are a Shedman.

I meet her cold stare now in genuine childish confusion, understanding neither the look nor the conversation, feeling the fear and dislike of these visits when we go on picnics so gaily and return silent. I make a great deal out of the eating of my cold chicken, speak with my mouth full, *I don't know what you're talking about, Pixie.*

You will. There's the best of reasons why it's the same thing, me giving Sam money and your grandfather selling the house. Bertram, are you listening to me?

Sure, sure, go ahead, listening and wishing I wasn't, thinking of the chicken and my toes in the wet crabgrass and the rough comfort of the blanket over the damp ground, afraid now that Pixie will insist on telling me what she is talking about, that she is going to descend into the workings of her thoughts and try to explain them.

They are the same thing because your grandfather didn't like to think about all those children, all the brothers and sisters he grew up with, all the other children he had to share the house with. When they were gone and he had the house he sold it to forget about them. Now do you understand? Do you?

No.

She waves my fright and curiosity away with a gesture and in disgust will not talk any more. I know this means she will be angry soon. I hope she will talk more, that always helps, but she won't, not about herself, not about the house, and not about the long dead husband, my grandfather, who now lies only a photograph on her desk, his forehead smeared a bright crayon orange, garishly staring at me not three feet from where I lie in Pixie's bed, while the nightwind slips in through her windows and ruffles her lace curtains and cools the heat of my concern.

Now on the hill in the stand of trees over the flowers the ten year old grandson and the fifty-six year old grandmother are silent, facing each other in quiet tension, adversaries for reasons the woman does not comprehend any better than the child. Even though he is a little boy, Pixie cannot keep the dark intensity of her glaring from becoming a reptilian coldness.

Pixie, what's wrong? Pixie?

It is as if I have disappeared, am no longer there at all. Pixie turns away and stares at the mountains to the west, beginning their arch and tumble and blue ascent a few miles from Maysville, clearly visible on this summer day. Her tiny hands, of which she has always been so justly proud, pick at the lace at her throat where the high necked blouse tucks itself under her chin. The hand suddenly cramps, as if stricken, and she claws nervously at her lace. She stands up and opens her collar, tears a button off, throws it on the ground, mutters to herself. She stamps a patent leather walking shoe on the ground, and she chokes out a shrill laughter.

Pixie?

Pixie?

Above me, looking down, the little waspish woman whose death has confused me as much as her life, glares at me, comes into focus with the finality and consistency of cooling metal.

Little fool. Little Shedman fool.

Pixie?

Pixie?

Her habitual wry and tolerant smile is gone, gone the dignity of her dark gaze. She kicks the lunch basket as I would have then kicked a football, away it goes tumbling, the wicker hinged covers flapping, the food spinning out onto the ground. She stamps her foot and tears at her matronly clothes, mourning among flowers and birches as I mourn for her now, lying in her bed, no longer frightened as I was then, when I scampered back away from her as she shook a ludicrous tiny white fist at the western mountains saying over and over *Fools fools fools.*

Then when I cannot help myself but begin to cry she comes partially back to herself, looks at me in bewilderment, and sees I am only myself, her grandson, and not responsible for being the incarnation of all Shedman men. It isn't, after all, my fault, and so

she goes after the lunch basket, picks it up and brings it back to me. She reaches inside it, and from the bottom, wrapped in cellophane, takes out a cap of fig leaves she had made for me, three leaves from an orchard of Maysville fig trees, laced together with pine straw, a rooster's comb of daisies that cascades down its back like a bridal veil. She holds it out to me, trembling on the brink of her angers, saying *Here Bertram here I made this for you Bertram honey* but I jump away angry myself and filled with my own rage, the anger of a child against the reasonless behavior of adults, demanding that such action be explained and expounded, coupled to actions that have preceded it, so that I will not, like her, become lost. In the open fierceness of childish self-protection I back away from Pixie's shattered thoughts, snarling, *No no get away from me with that thing.*

The fig leaf bridal veiled cap held out, she looks at me bleakly. The cold reptilian stare is gone, replaced by the gaze of a tourist in a strange and uninteresting city, bored beyond boredom, crushed by a waste of time and money and a cruel disappointment of expectation. *Bertram don't be like that here come on I made this for you take it*

No

Bertram Shedman you take this I mean it you take it

You're crazy get away from me Pixie you're crazy

And then I was no longer myself but every bit of every Shedman man and she tried to hit me, swung her tiny hand, aimed her delicate arm in a swift but useless swing, and I backed away so quickly that she almost fell over. She regains her balance, and stares at me as if I had tried to hit her.

What are you trying to do Pixie kill me?

What, son?

You tried to hit me do you want to kill me then?

No no no no no no

And her mad gaze then all about us darting here and there as if to see something she can grasp, something that can hold her rooted down from a threat of whirlwinds. I crouch in front of her as if I were back in school and fighting on the playground and she takes as much breath as she can, saying, *Look Bertram wait a minute and look with me now*

Stay there don't you try to hit me again

I won't oh I won't

And standing there with me crouching in front of her with my fists doubled my grandmother simply begins to talk, quietly, with only the rush of her words betraying her, and my absurd crouch and fists testament of the violence between an old woman and a little boy. She talks to me about the mountains she has cursed, and tells me they are like stockades that shut people in until they are afraid ever to go out of them, and if they do go out they carry that fear with them forever. It is a fear, she tells me, of tiny small things for they are a people surrounded by gigantic peaks yet acquainted with the infinitely little. I do not understand her but I stand up and let my fists uncurl. She turns then and points to the east, to the small hills that run down into flatland and move eventually to the sea, to the Atlantic coast and the Hatteras reef where she was a child, points and in her release of herself before me talks about the seas and the grandmother even I can see is vanishing before me, a young woman is speaking with rapture and yearning. And I stand up straight, hands at my side, looking where she points over the town of Maysville, as if I can see in that drab small-town landscape gulls and sand and sea-oats, cresting breakers, foam and unlimited space.

Abruptly, she breaks it off. Her rhapsody recoils against her and she turns, angry again, to the Shedman male who will not know what she is talking about, who will think her crazy and say so, with whom

she must do battle to preserve the life she has lived. She holds up the fig leaf cap with spiteful shame, ready to throw it to the ground or at me, and chews her thin lips in mortification. I did not understand her then, I do not understand her now, but my instincts were conquered. I did not run away from her or continue my defiance, but faced what all my childhood told me I should flee, and I let her put on my head the cap of fig leaves, and told her, *Oh Pixie, you certainly do know a lot of things about the seaside, don't you.* Then, as her mask of pain and exhausting rage cracked apart, caught for a moment in Pixie's arms under a clear Carolina sky, in a mad rhapsody of cold chicken and bright crabgrass, standing barefoot in the ease of loose-clodded earth, in that incredible villanelle of flowers and birch trees I embraced her with love, entering in childhood the tangled adult confusion from which I am descended.

FROM

THE NIGHT OF THE GERMAN MAN

BY RALPH SMITH

Henry Roux's knife trimmed away the outer gristle of the steak, pushing the opaque lumps neatly to the side of the platter.

"Best damn steak in the world," he grunted, suddenly looking up into my eyes. "You know we haven't seen each other in seven years. You're just as skinny as you ever were. How's that steak? You know what Abe does to that meat? He gets a whole side of prime Omaha beef and ages it until the outside is green with fuzz. Then it's fit to eat—juicy and sweet."

Henry Roux bent again to his food, soft jowls cracking on lettuce and hard roll. Beyond the restaurant's dark interior three Negro boys played tag on the sidewalk. Henry Roux ate silently, carving the pink and black meat with smooth strokes, digging at a stuffed potato festered with rich cheese, toying with his jungle of salad. Suddenly he stopped eating and picked up a newspaper from the seat of the booth. He glanced quickly through it, waiting for his stomach to belch. "I can't even read a goddam newspaper any more," he said, throwing the paper aside. "China, niggers, missiles, and more taxes. We pay and the po' folks ride." A tiny driblet of beef blood filled a pock mark on the edge of Henry Roux's lips.

"Let me tell you something. You ever hear that joke about the nigger being buried alive? Some manufacturer's representative from Mississippi told it. Those people down there'll tell you anything. Anyway it seems the Klan got hold of a nigger one night and took him out in the country and started whipping him. They beat him with jackhandles, belts, chain, anything they could get their hands on, but they

couldn't kill him. Big bluegum nigger. So the deputy sheriff in charge gave the problem some thought and decided to bury the nigger up to his neck and then sic his dog on him. So they dug this hole and put the bluegum down in it and filled it up with dirt and tamped it down good around his neck. . . . This coffee's cold again. Goddam air-conditioning makes it cold. . . . Anyway, the sheriff turned his dog loose and said 'get 'im boy' and the dog ran at the nigger. When the dog got there the bluegum reached up and bit half the dog's head off and spit it out. So the deputy sheriff hit him in the head with a shovel and said to him, 'Fight fair, nigger.' " Henry Roux giggled softly.

Darkness mingled with the afternoon light beyond the windows. Clouds passed overhead, throwing shadows on the buildings across the street.

"I forgot to tell you about that Cornish hen recipe I picked up in Atlanta," Henry Roux said. "Beautiful eating. Just clean and stuff a Cornish hen with a mixture of wild rice and *paté de fois gras*—get the kind that's as pink as a gal's nipple. Use a little white pepper and salt and a white wine butter basting. Serve it with asparagus. Best goddam stuff you'll ever put in your mouth. Good. Here's some hot coffee."

The waitress appeared with two silex carafes of coffee. "What's your name, dear?" Henry Roux asked. "Ann. Very pretty name. Tell Abe Henry Roux from Prudential was asking about him." The girl smiled and walked away. "Look at that," Henry Roux said. "Look at that fanny under that goddam black silk skirt. . . . Abe keeps some nice-looking women here."

He turned his coffee light brown with several wax containers of cream.

"I knew a gal once looked like her, up in York County somewhere. Back when I was selling insurance on debit, which reminds me of another story. Did I tell you? We had this turd in the office who always wore double-breasted suits and had bad breath. I remember that. Well, his first day collecting debit accounts, he went up to this gal's house and asked her for the 63 cents she owed that week. She took him upstairs, pulled up her dress and asked him if he wanted to take it out in trade like the rest of us did. He *demanded* his 63 cents, and got mad at the woman. Came running back to the office red in the face and complained about her. Best piece he'll ever run up against, and he's mad. Anyway, getting back to York County, I picked up this young thing on Route 322. She was crying and standing there, so I just scooped her up and headed for the woods. Some damn story about missing her bus to Lancaster. Trouble is you don't know about those girls. They look twelve till they're twenty and then they look fifty till they're dead. Anyway I got her in the back seat and put it to her. She smelled like an old Indian gal I knew once down at Pembroke—made my eyes water. Anyway I just let her out of the car after I finished and backed out of the dirt road so she couldn't read my license number. She just stood there, eyes all puffy—didn't even know what hit her."

Henry Roux touched his high silk collar and pawed at the air. The waitress brought two pieces of crusted apple pie covered with pistachios and butter. Henry Roux munched silently on the dessert, toying with the pistachios.

"We're just too good to niggers down here," he said. "They come out of those little jigaboo colleges and expect to take over everything. Nigger car-hop I know in Columbia, working his way through college, was boasting about his teacher being the smartest man in the world. He could write on the blackboard with both hands, the nigger said, write different things with each hand. How's that for genius? Then they walk out of a school like that and expect to be Governor of the goddam state. . . . Don't leave, Clai, for Christ's sake. Still a hundred degrees out there. Have some more of Abe's coffee. He makes it from mocha java, Blue Mountain and that good stuff they grow in Hawaii. . . . Reminds me of the coffee we used to have at home, when Momma was living. . . . You know I keep staring at that waitress and I do believe she's got the most pumped-up ass I ever seen on a white woman. Look at her. No fat behind the knees. Gal with a big ass and no fat behind the knees is my kind."

He stuck his finger into the coffee and watched it drip back into the cup.

"We had an old colored gal working for us back then, when Momma was living. Big old fat gal who cooked the best cabbage in the world. Just a touch of vinegar to keep the cabbage red and great big chunks of black pepper and dill. Effie. She stayed with us right on through the Depression, when there wasn't a pot to pee in down here. Had to pay her in food for five straight years, I remember.

"Anyway she finally started stealing. Stole this old rusty Lucky Strike box they used to make before the war. Red and green box Momma kept her buttons in. Stole a lot of things nobody really wanted. Then I remember one day she stuck a clump of celery behind this wood stove we had at the house. Momma caught her and told her 'well, I'd have given you the celery if you'd asked, Effie,' and the goddam celery was all black with smoke grease and Effie standing there looking sad. I knew she'd tell on me. Momma used to go off every Saturday morning and me and Effie would be by ourselves. I knew she'd say something but she didn't. She just took the celery and walked out the door and we never saw her again. . . . Have you seen *The Guns of Navarone?* Best goddam movie ever made. I've seen it four times already. . . ."

Henry Roux returned from the restroom and collapsed into the booth. His fingernails were no longer streaked with grease and blood. He smelled faintly of Chanel shaving lotion, which he carried in a small container in his coat. Glancing toward the kitchen entrance where the waitresses were sitting idly, he dug at his ear and smelled his finger.

"I'm getting off the road, Clai. I been on the road ever since we were discharged. Made a lot of money. See this suit? Bernard Weatherill Limited. See how the cuff buttons really button and unbutton? We sure were poor bastards in Tokyo. Couldn't even scrape up enough money to get one of us laid. Remember that weekend? Anyway I'm not seeing my family enough. Paid $12,000 for a summer house on Lake Tahl and I've slept in it five nights. Stay on the goddam road all the time and next week we start having a weekly sales conference on Saturday morning. I've been in the Million Dollar Roundtable Sales Club for three years straight and they want *me* to attend some goddam weekly sales meeting. . . . So I just might take the inside job they're offering me."

The Negro children were still playing in front of the restaurant window, juggling pieces of hickory kept in front for the charcoal fires. Henry Roux signaled the waitress, who returned with two carafes of fresh coffee. "Honey, those kids out there are going to break Abe's window if they don't watch out." He rubbed the girl's arm as she poured his coffee. The screeches of the Negro children carried like damp forest noises into the restaurant. The waitress began clearing the table.

"You know, Clai, this is one fine looking woman here. Wouldn't she be something walking around on the Hilton Head beach—maybe in one of those fine black bathing suits they sell at Montaldo's. . . . I'm going down to Charleston next weekend, Ann—or rather this coming weekend. I never have figured out what people mean when they say 'next weekend.' Maybe I could just interest you in a vacation for a couple of days. We'd just run down, do some shopping while we're there, eat at Perdita's and head for the beach. Charleston is something this time of year, isn't it, Clai?" He stared at me as though I had left five minutes before. "Really something. Maybe we could just relax and get brown and have a good time. Hell, I'm not going to mess you up, honey."

The waitress ignored him. A faint smile curled her thin lips.

"Nobody has to know, Ann. Is it Ann? Nobody has to know. Are you worried about Abe finding out? Hell, Abe's just another restaurant owner. I could get you a job in the finest restaurant in the south—anywhere you want to work."

Henry Roux's face glowed and fattened as he leaned forward. He stared at her skirt. He wondered what he could give her. He would have given her his children.

Suddenly she turned away, her pinched face sweeping past me to the street beyond, where shadows fell over the buildings, mottling the passing cars.

She walked back to the booth where the other waitresses were sitting and soon they were laughing.

Henry Roux stared at the wet table. "You know what I'd like to do? I'd like to throw her down and watch her eyes pop out. Make her crawl. Giving me that silent business." He took his glass of water and carefully laid a paper napkin over the rim, then turned it upside down on the table. "That'll fix her smart ass," Henry Roux said. "Let her try to pick up that glass of water without spilling it all over the goddam floor."

He giggled, distressed, then carefully drew all of his grief back inside. "Did I tell you about that recipe I picked up in Atlanta? I told you about that? About the wild rice and the *paté de fois gras* . . .?"

· ·

Escape

The line-snake
begins its undulating dance
in the drug-induced fog.
My shaking head
refocuses the skimming yellow wave,
As the car streaks through the night

                           to the peace of hell.

An eerie whine from the distance
brings the flying breathlessness to a lump
which floors the accelerator.
. . . 70 . . . 90 . . . 100 . . .

Fleeing not the red light screeching around the curve
But the stranger,
compulsively driven by the unrequitable demon within.

In a curse of realism,
I know I am the driver.

The thin line snaps
As the speedometer
               drops
           past
          120 . . .

Betty R. Ford

"HEAD"   GILBERT CARPENTER

RESPONSE

In this section some of the contributors comment on their work—or decline to comment, in the case of Jasper Johns—and a reader expresses an opinion.

I'd like to say something about this story, "To Whom Shall I Call Now in My Hour of Need." Anyway, I owe a word or two of explanation. I've been working at this story in various forms and versions for some years. It's been a couple of unpublished novels and one unproduced play. Some things in it—though they involve different people and a different place—appear in a new novel called *Do, Lord, Remember Me*. Some things in it will be in another novel not yet finished. But in neither case is the story a part of something else. It is, I hope, complete of and by itself. I'm tired of the little short story with a single vivid event and one point of view. I like to think we are all only beginning to explore the territory and that the form can stand the strain of testing and exploration. I am very happy to have this story in RED CLAY where a writer can try some things he hasn't done before and see what happens. I hope that what happens is that some readers will enjoy it.

GEORGE GARRETT

I have examined RED CLAY READER with steadily increasing interest and appreciation. It seems to me that you are speaking in the idiom of an intelligent esthetics—not a tautology, for the esthetic of idiocy is omnipresent—but with a well-defined Tarheel accent.

To be regional without being parochial is quite an achievement, but I think you have made it. Inevitably, I compare your effort with that of Emily Clark (later Balch) forty years ago. Mencken constantly yammered at Emily to get more of Virginia and less of England and France into *The Reviewer*. He was right; but I don't think he would make the same criticism of RED CLAY READER. I think, therefore, that you are a step in advance.

I think of an argument that, as Voltaire said of God, if North Carolina did not exist it would be necessary to invent it. Perhaps we have. If Boston is a state of mind, so is any culture; the task is to cultivate, perhaps to cross-pollinate what already grows wild in the soil until "the flowers turn double and the leaves turn flowers."

GERALD JOHNSON

When I go back to North Carolina, where I was born and raised, I'm always struck, having become accustomed to the language of another region, by the grace of the cadences of North Carolina speech. I tried in these two said-songs first of all to acknowledge that I did not write them so much as "overhear" them, and second, and consequently, to reproduce the speech as faithfully as I could. It seemed to me that these two speeches made wholes naturally, whole motions, so

RESPONSE

that it was easy for me to remember them approximately as they were said. I'm not, though, specially bent on reproducing natural speech: poems that find artificial cadences in artificial language can be as authentic and powerful as any.

A. R. AMMONS

The drawings which appear in this issue are by artists from and/or living in this area. The work was selected primarily on the basis of quality and represents some current and varied approaches.

MAUD GATEWOOD

I tend to reject any talk about painting because it scares people off and talk is too often used as a means of evading the issue of looking at painting.

JASPER JOHNS

The pressures confronting the Negro writer usually are connected with his position as an American Negro. Primarily, as other writers, he has to decide upon his subject matter and the means by which he will publish his work. Then, he is faced with the added problem of maintaining his integrity as a writer in an era when involvement in civl rights is a popular cause.

With the current interest in the freedom movement, many readers automatically assume that civil rights is the topic of the colored author's work. Often a Negro is expected to be an angry writer; that he may want to write about quiet situations without a message is surprising. Most of us have encountered situations whereby someone wants to "discover" a Negro. The general feeling in these instances is that a non-rebel without a cause might as well not be black.

Of course a person tends to write about the things with which he is familiar, and most Negroes are familiar with occurences within the Negro community. Yet he does not want to limit his writing to correspond with another person's expectations. Last semester one of my classmates expressed discontent with a professor because "he wants me to write black." For the next few years I imagine that jumping on the civil rights bandwagon and writing about the cause will be a major temptation, even if a person's interests are varied. Social protest literature is a part of the American literary tradition, but I would much rather editorialize in an editorial, and not in fiction.

Writing should be judged according to the intrinsic value. During the Harlem Renaissance of the 1920's praising a colored author's work was part of a popular movement. Again in the 60's when attention is focused on the Negro, we have to make certain our writing is judged according to regular literary standards. Diluting standards in accordance with a person's race does not help strengthen his writing. Honest criticism is an important part of this craft; and as a Negro writer I certainly do not want my work to be judged as an exception to the rule.

DIANE OLIVER

I am very pleased that the first thing of mine to receive any serious consideration anywhere, made it with you, because I feel that your first RED CLAY READER was good, and even more important, it was human. I mean I got a feeling of what it is you are trying to do, and of what the writers who contributed to it were trying to say.

As for the biographical information you requested, it will have to be brief, because if it isn't then I might succumb to the urge to write a life story, since this is the first personal response I have ever received from any editor regarding my submissions and I am ego-filled with all kinds of self-laudatory pride.

TOM WEATHERS

At the ripe old age of twenty-one I like to think that I will be able to do something about the things that bother me so much. Then I look again and see that actually there is quite a lot going on that I did not take into consideration the first time that would be more than glad to crush me like a fly. From this comes a heavy dose of the cynical in my work, tempered by a distraught optimism. My work is just that to me, mine, my personal explanation and answer to what is important. I do not intentionally pick a controversial topic and prepare a protest poem on it like a grocer marking cabbages. Poetry is to me, and I think it should be, a result of stimulus uncontrolled by the writer. The words form his view, but the stimulus is outside him.

I am, of course, obviously protesting, but I am not carrying a picket sign saying same, nor am I wearing a hooded bedsheet or trying to impeach Earl Warren. I am decrying the plight of people, hoping to open their eyes and their minds. This is to me, in Damon Runyon's words, "a very big deal."

My disgust with segregationists, commercialized religion, etc., is no greater than the disgust I hold for the big-time, money-making, lapel-button collecting, self-righteous, professional protestors. They run their own class ridden society under the banner of individualism. My writing purposely takes these bigots into account because they seem more intentionally hypocritical than the uneducated who are caught up in racism, evangelism, and super-patriotism. My derision preferably comes out in poetry, not riots or sit-ins.

No matter how minute my protest may be, or is thought to be, it is nevertheless mine. My main intention at the moment is to try to continue writing the way I feel and want, without stylizing my way into one camp or another. My ultimate aim is to not have to write "protest poetry," but to get on with being more poetic, being a romantic at heart anyway.

JOEL JACKSON

THE CONTRIBUTORS

A. R. Ammons was born in Whiteville, North Carolina. His poems have appeared in *Hudson Review* and *Partisan Review*, and he is the author of four volumes, two of which appeared in 1965: *Corsons Inlet* and *Tape for the Turn of the Year*.

Gilbert Carpenter has taught at the University of Hawaii and Columbia University. He is currently Chairman of the Art Department at the University of North Carolina at Greensboro. He has had one-man shows in San Francisco and New York.

Fred Chappell has written two widely acclaimed novels since 1963. Born in the mountains of North Carolina, he is now teaching at the University of North Carolina at Greensboro.

CHAPPELL

Judson Crews earns his living as a printer in Taos, New Mexico. He was born in Texas and keeps up the courage of little magazine editors across the country by circulating a goodly number of his good poems.

CREWS

Harriet Doar is on the arts staff of *The Charlotte Observer*. Her poetry has appeared in various magazines and "The Fighting Cocks" is her first published fiction.

Charles East was born in Mississippi and is now the editor of Louisiana State University Press. His stories have been published in *Mademoiselle, Yale Review,* and *Virginia Quarterly,* and his first volume, *Where the Music Was,* has been recently published by Harcourt, Brace & World.

DOAR

Deborah Eibel was born in 1940. She has taught at the University of North Carolina and her poems have appeared in several little magazines.

Betty R. Ford also was born in 1940, in South Carolina. She majored in physical education in Virginia and is now settled down with two children and two horses in Hickory, North Carolina. "Escape" is the first poem she has had published.

EAST

Edsel Ford comes from Alabama. He has received several awards for poetry, recorded for the Library of Congress, and directed poetry workshops for the University of Kansas writers conference.

George Garrett is the author of nine books, seven published when he was between the ages of 28 and 32. A poet, a novelist, author of three volumes of short stories, Mr. Garrett also writes for the stage and screen. He spent last year as Writer-in-Residence at Princeton University and has this year returned to teaching at the University of Virginia.

FORD

GARRETT

GATEWOOD

GREEN

JACKSON

KEROUAC

MAUD GATEWOOD produced several of the drawings in her portfolio while on a Fulbright scholarship to Vienna. She is chairman of the art department at the University of North Carolina at Charlotte.

RICHARD GOLDHURST's first novel, *The Deceivers*, has recently gone into its third printing. Mr. Goldhurst lives in Westport, Connecticut, and is the associate editor of *The Carolina Israelite*.

PAUL GREEN is a Pulitzer Prize winner and widely known as the author of many outdoor dramas including *The Lost Colony* and *The Common Glory*. He also has written many screen plays in Hollywood but is locally considered the Southern writer with a heart and a helping hand.

A. HILL writes that she was born, survived, went to school, taught, retired, went back to school, retired again, and is now at work surviving in Walnut Cove, North Carolina.

JOEL JACKSON is a student trying to double major in philosophy and English. He gives account of himself in the "Response" section and his lively poems are on page 49.

JASPER JOHNS was born in Georgia, but grew up in South Carolina. He has become famous and has had numerous one-man shows in America, Europe, and Japan. He now lives and works at Edisto Beach.

JACK KEROUAC is the author of *On the Road*. He rides the RED CLAY READER editor on page 48.

WALTER KERR works for the United States Government. He writes that an awareness of poetry as a vocation came to him in France during World War II and his poems have subsequently appeared in a score of little magazines and several anthologies.

ROMULUS LINNEY is on the faculty of the Manhattan School of Music. His first novel, *Heathen Valley*, was set in the North Carolina mountains and his second novel, *Slowly, By Thy Hand Unfurled*, has been called brilliant. RED CLAY READER is proud to publish a part of his novel in progress.

MACKEY is a painter who also has taught. Her work has been exhibited in the South and she is currently curator for the Winston-Salem Gallery.

CLARENCE MAJOR was the editor of *Coercion* which he reports defunct. He lives in Omaha, Nebraska, and his work has appeared in many anthologies and little magazines including *Black Orpheus, Literary Review,* and *Negro Digest*.

ADRIANNE MARCUS is a North Carolina poet who is living in California.

HEATHER ROSS MILLER studied with Randall Jarrell and her poetry appeared in the first issue of RED CLAY READER. She is also a novelist whose first book, *Edge of the Woods*, was highly praised and whose second novel will be published in 1966. Mrs. Miller lives with her husband and two children at Singletary Lake State Park in North Carolina.

MILLER

PAUL NEWMAN was born in Chicago. He has taught at Kansas State and the University of Puerto Rico and is now teaching at Queens College in Charlotte, North Carolina. His poems have appeared in *Poetry, Chicago Review, Prairie Schooner*, and other magazines.

KATHRYN NOYES' first novel, *Jacob's Ladder*, was released by Bobbs-Merrill in the Spring of 1965. Born in Boston, educated in California, Mrs. Noyes lives in Durham, North Carolina, with her four children, and has completed her second book, *From Time Memorial*.

OLIVER

DIANE OLIVER is twenty-two and her first published work appears in this issue of RED CLAY READER. A native of Charlotte, North Carolina, Miss Oliver is now on a writing scholarship at the University of Iowa.

ENNIS REES, who is the author of several scholarly works as well as a poet, has also done a verse translation of the *Iliad* and the *Odyssey* for Modern Library. A professor of English at the University of South Carolina, Mr. Rees was born in Virginia.

REES

WILLIAM ROBINSON is a professor of English at the University of Virginia and is at work on a study of recent short fiction to be published by Louisiana State University Press.

H. ROTH lives in Laurel Hill, New York, and has recently finished a volume of short stories. "Der Tag" is the second story to be published from that collection.

ROTH

RALPH SMITH is an editorial writer now living and working in Washington, D. C. He is at work on his novel to be called "The Night of the German Man." The excerpt included in this issue of RED CLAY READER is his first published fiction.

DABNEY STUART has won several prizes and published widely since his appearance in the first issue of RED CLAY READER. The recipient of the Dylan Thomas Award, Mr. Stuart's first volume will be published by Knopf in 1966.

SMITH

TOM WEATHERS, JR., was born and raised in Shelby, North Carolina. "The Mill" is his first published fiction.